"Is something wrong?"

"Uh-uh." Elise shook her head, still watching him. "I think the baby just moved."

"It's probably indigestion," he said. "You're only four months along. That's too soon, isn't it?"

"Not with quads. [...] I'm already show[...] happen at four [...]

Elise felt herself [...] as she asked, sta[...] her stomach.

"There it is again!" she cried out, grinning, feeling idiotically close to tears. "I'm sure that's the baby moving. I've never felt anything like it before!"

"Let me feel."

She'd barely registered the words before Joe's larger, warmer hand was pushing hers aside and flattening against her stomach. She wanted to tell him it was too soon to feel anything on the outside, but his hand felt so good. So right.

She was *so* in trouble.

Dear Reader,

Happy holidays! Have you ever wanted something so badly that you can't stop thinking about it? So badly that you're compelled to do whatever it takes to make it happen? That's kind of how things went with this book. When I met Elise she was going to have quadruplets. That's all I knew about her. I'd seen this quad stroller while I was out shopping one day last fall and when the questions started coming, I knew I was going to have to write a story about a multiple birth. That was when Elise appeared.

And then, as usually happens in my world, emotions started to appear from nowhere and take over *my* story. I fought them a bit. Tried to tell them who was really boss. But once I conceded that I *wasn't* the one in charge here, a story unfolded that I think will touch your heart. It has certainly touched mine.

In each of us is a drive to achieve something, whether that be financial, emotional, career based, relationship based, or something else entirely. We all have needs. This is the story of someone just like us–a woman whose heart cries out for more. For love and belonging. But with Elise, it doesn't stop with the wanting. She steps outside the normal boundaries of societal expectations to provide her life with the fullness she craves. Her journey is lonely. It isn't easy, by any stretch. And in the end, being true to herself and the dictates of her heart–she is successful. Beyond her dreams.

I learned an important lesson from Elise Richardson. I don't have to settle. This holiday season, my gift to you is the challenge to ask yourself for more. And then to make it happen… Next Christmas, we can check back with each other to see what we've accomplished!

Tara Taylor Quinn

MERRY CHRISTMAS, BABIES

Tara Taylor Quinn

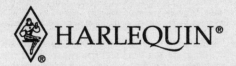

TORONTO • NEW YORK • LONDON
AMSTERDAM • PARIS • SYDNEY • HAMBURG
STOCKHOLM • ATHENS • TOKYO • MILAN • MADRID
PRAGUE • WARSAW • BUDAPEST • AUCKLAND

ISBN-13: 978-0-373-71381-3
ISBN-10:   0-373-71381-9

MERRY CHRISTMAS, BABIES

Copyright © 2006 by Tara Taylor Quinn.

This edition published by arrangement with Harlequin Books S.A.

® and TM are trademarks of the publisher. Trademarks indicated with ® are registered in the United States Patent and Trademark Office, the Canadian Trade Marks Office and in other countries.

www.eHarlequin.com

Printed in U.S.A.

ABOUT THE AUTHOR

Tara's first book, *Yesterday's Secrets,* published in October 1993, was a finalist for the Romance Writers of America's prestigious RITA® Award. Her subsequent work has earned her finalist status for the National Readers' Choice Award and the Holt Medallion, plus another two RITA® Award nominations. A prolific writer, she has forty-two novels and three novellas published. To reach Tara write to her at P.O. Box 133584, Mesa, Arizona 85216 or through her Web site, www.tarataylorquinn.com.

Books by Tara Taylor Quinn

HARLEQUIN SUPERROMANCE
1057–THE SECRET SON
1087–THE SHERIFF OF SHELTER VALLEY*
1135–BORN IN THE VALLEY*
1171–FOR THE CHILDREN
1189–NOTHING SACRED*
1225–WHAT DADDY DOESN'T KNOW
1272–SOMEBODY'S BABY*
1297–25 YEARS
(anthology with Margot Early & Janice Macdonald)
1309–THE PROMISE OF CHRISTMAS
1350–A CHILD'S WISH

HARLEQUIN SINGLE TITLE
SHELTERED IN HIS ARMS*

*Shelter Valley Stories

MIRA BOOKS
WHERE THE ROAD ENDS
STREET SMART
HIDDEN
IN PLAIN SIGHT

For Rachel—my dearest gift. If you only ever learn one thing from me, please let it be always to listen to your heart and act as it directs.

CHAPTER ONE

"ANYONE HEAR FROM ELISE?" Joe Bennett walked into the lunchroom at the back of the suite of offices he and his partner—and the bank—now owned. Eating meals ranging from fruit and yogurt to homemade burgers, the employees Elise Richardson supervised sat at the long, elegant wooden table.

"Not a word." Twenty-five-year-old Angela Parks glanced over her shoulder at him from the granite-topped island marking the center of the full kitchen on one end of the room. She was making a salad.

It was Thursday. On Fridays Elise cooked lunch for their nine-member staff. Maybe she was out grocery shopping for the next day's offering.

But it would be the first time in the ten years they'd been in business that she'd done so during the workday. At night, while Joe left the job and lived a life, Elise worked at home—or shopped for the office.

"She didn't say where she was going?"

"I think she had a dentist appointment," Ruth Gregory said, straightening a stem in the silk flower centerpiece in front of her. At fifty, she was the oldest B&R employee.

"No." Thirty-five-year-old Mark Oppenheimer popped the last of his usual peanut butter sandwich in his mouth and stood. "That was last month. Today she didn't say what kind of appointment, only that she shouldn't be gone more than an hour."

"What time was that?"

"Nine." As their chief financial officer, the skinny, bespectacled man was Elise's second in command and the source most likely to be up to date.

Glancing at his multi-dialed designer watch—which his then-wife had bought him for Christmas a few years ago and which Joe wore because it would be a waste not to, even though he preferred the simple large-faced cheap number he'd worn in college—he frowned.

"That was almost four hours ago."

Mark wiped the crumbs he'd left on the table onto the floor—a man after his own heart. "I know," he said.

"And she hasn't called?"

"No."

After another few seconds of standing there blankly, Joe started to leave. And then turned back.

"Anyone think to call the hospitals to make sure she wasn't in an accident?" He was only half joking, but their chuckles followed him down the hallway.

"I've got lunch with Anderson, Anderson and Bailey," he told his secretary on his way out. The law firm was the biggest in the state of Michigan— a six-million-dollar account—and B&R had been courting them for a couple of years. "Text message me the second Elise gets in, will you?"

Bennett and Richardson Professional Employee Organization, or B&R PEO, offered companies a comprehensive package that included payroll, workers' compensation, tax compliance and group insurance, all at a rate lower than they could arrange for themselves. Joe Bennett was in charge of sales, and Elise Richardson, his best friend from college, oversaw virtually everything else.

Normally his cell phone was in the Off position when he was in meetings—commonly disguised as social gatherings now that he had two salesmen who made the office calls to sit with managers and work out logistics. Today he turned his cell on to Vibrate instead, so he'd know if and when a message came through. He didn't have an urgent need to speak to his business partner. He just wanted to assure himself that she was going to be around at some point to nag him about something.

THE LONG, FAMILIAR private road across the front of the cemetery was potholed and narrow, barely wide enough to fit the Corvette. Elise passed several lanes that sectioned off areas filled with headstones of varying sizes, many with urns bearing colorful floral arrangements planted on Memorial Day two and a half weeks before. As she rounded the back border of the carefully tended green acreage, she slowed to a stop, then climbed out of the car, wrapping her short, three-quarter-sleeved white sweater more closely around her.

She'd thought this stage of her life was about moving on. Becoming.

Yet it turned out, at the moment, she needed her family.

Concentrating on the feel of the soft, cool grass, Elise walked barefoot toward the stone bearing her family name. It brought a happy memory of running through the grass in bare feet, chasing her older brother—because if she could catch him, he'd let her ride on the back of his bike to go for an ice cream cone.

Back then, she'd thought that she'd always managed to catch him because she was so strong and fast. Now she understood that he'd allowed her to. And she smiled.

"Hi," she said.

Tucking her calf-length, white-and-pink floral cotton skirt beneath her, she sat directly in front of the main stone marked Richardson. And didn't know what else to say. Normally her visits were to take care of their gravesites—pull weeds, plant flowers, scrub their stones. And while she worked, she'd tell them about the business, something that happened with an employee or a new building in town—not that they'd ever even heard of Lowell, Michigan.

She'd bought the plot and buried what was left of their ashes, brought with her from Arkansas, as part of her therapy about eight years before.

"Mama?"

Her voice broke when she heard the word come out of her mouth. So she turned to another of the individual stones, bearing first and middle names, birth and death dates. "Daddy?"

It wasn't any easier. Her gaze moved again. "Danny?"

And again. "Ellen?"

"Baby Grace?"

There'd been four of them once. Four children filling her parents' home and hearts.

Now there was only her.

And...

"Mama?" She cried openly because she couldn't help it, and because there was no one around to see. Wiping her eyes with the bottom edge of her skirt, she finally admitted, "I'm scared."

Complete silence followed the confession. Inside of her and out.

"I'm scared, Mama," she said again, more firmly. "I know I'm not supposed to be, that I'm a survivor, but sometimes I wish I'd died along with the rest of you."

She quieted, waited to be struck for the ungrateful thought. But nothing happened. She wasn't punished. And the thought didn't leave, either.

"Why did I have to be the one they got? Why did my bedroom have to be on the farthest side of the house? Why did Ellen share a room with Grace and not me? Why only me?"

Because you're special.

The words were a whisper in her mind, almost as though carried on the light breeze. They were a memory from her early childhood. And from the physically and emotionally agonizing months and years that stretched from her eleventh year to her twentieth. She'd lost track of the number of people who'd said the words to her.

But she could still hear them in her mother's voice the day she'd asked her why she couldn't have been the oldest like Danny, or the first girl like Ellen, or the baby like Grace. She'd been searching for her place, even then, stuck in the middle with no solid sense of how she fit.

She stared at the smaller stone bearing her mother's name. Wanting. Wishing. Needing.

"I'm pregnant, Mama."

The stone in front of her blurred again. Pulling her knees up, her arms wrapped around them, Elise sat still and let her life settle around her as it would. And as the tears continued to flow, she lifted the edge of her skirt a second time, wiping her face. A face that none of the people whose names were engraved on those small, cold stones would ever recognize.

JOE WASN'T SURE what to think when, at five after six that Thursday evening in mid-June, he walked up the steps of his partner's elegant, colonial-style home on Lakeshore Drive overlooking the Flat River and knocked on the door. She pulled it open, looking as normal and fine as she did any other day.

"You're okay." He hadn't meant to sound disappointed. Hell, he wasn't! He was relieved as hell. But—

"I'm fine."

"You haven't missed a day of work since we opened shop ten years ago."

"Then I guess I was due."

"You didn't call." Sweating in his short-sleeved shirt and tie, although the evening was a balmy seventy degrees, Joe shifted from foot to foot.

"I own the company, Joe. I don't have to call."

She was right, of course. "Co-own."

"How many times have *you* missed coming into the office and not called in about it?" Her chin lifted a notch, her dark, short, sassy hair falling away from her neck.

It was different for him. He made outside calls. And even when he took a day off... "I take my cell phone everywhere. You can always reach me if there's an emergency."

"I had mine, too."

"You didn't answer."

"I listened to the messages."

Then she realized he'd been checking to make

sure she was okay. And she hadn't bothered to call him back, to assure him that she was.

Odd.

"Can I come in?"

She hesitated and then nodded, stepping away from the door.

He followed her through the formal living room, dining room and kitchen to the family room in the back of the house. He'd never understood why a woman who lived alone wanted so much space around her, but then, he'd never understood Elise, period.

Outside the office, that was.

A half-filled and perspiring glass of what appeared to be mostly juice and melted ice sat on the end table. The lamp was on. The large-screen television in front of the creamy white leather sofa was silent. There were no books, remote controls, or papers to indicate that his partner had been doing anything while she'd been sitting there.

Tucking her feet beneath her white skirt, she curled up on the sofa. And picked at her fingernails.

Her cats, Darin and Samantha, settled behind her on the back of the sofa.

"You mind if I get myself a bottle of water?" He wasn't thirsty. Except, perhaps, for a shot of bourbon. Straight up.

He hadn't consumed alcohol straight up since college.

"Of course not." Her smoky gray eyes were

more mysterious to him than usual as she glanced at him. Why did the woman's expression so rarely show him what she was thinking, like everyone else's did? "Help yourself."

Retrieving a bottle from the top shelf of the refrigerator, he glanced around the kitchen. The red-and-gold-flowered canisters that matched the wall paper border topping the golden accent wall were all neatly in place. Salt and pepper shakers that went with the set were on the stove where he'd always seen them in the past. If she'd eaten anything, she'd already cleaned up. And dried the sink, as well.

She'd had Kelly and him for dinner on a regular basis when they'd still been married. Joe couldn't remember her ever drying out the sink when she'd finished the dishes.

Hadn't she eaten?

"So what'd you do today?" He tried for casual as he approached her again, unsure whether he should join her on the couch or remain standing.

Now her eyes were moist when she looked at him, as though, while he'd been perusing her kitchen, she'd been crying. Or was about to start.

This was new ground for him. In the almost fourteen years they'd known each other it had somehow always been *her* picking up the pieces for *him*. He stared at the polished gleam on his wing-tip shoes.

"Mostly I stayed home."

Joe thought about the times *he'd* taken off work—they weren't as rare as hers, but rare enough that the hours were filled to the brim.

"Mostly?"

Elise's smile settled his nerves some. "It's okay, Joe. You can go. I'm fine. Really."

He wanted to go.

"You sure you're okay?"

She nodded. Darin opened one eye and closed it again.

Joe drank the bottle of water, recapped it, planning to throw it in the trash in the kitchen on his way out. He had a frozen Salisbury steak and mashed potato dinner to get home to. And then was meeting a couple of bankers for drinks at nine, after their racquetball game. If all went well, he'd be signing on their chain of financial institutions, Michigan Local Banks, to begin payroll at the beginning of July. It was a ten-million-dollar account—a hundred-thousand-dollar-a-year payout to B&R—his largest yet.

Joe glanced at his partner, the woman who'd been his buddy in college, challenging his thinking at every turn, challenging him to put his money where his mouth was and go into business, intimidating the hell out of him a time or two, listening to him whine and then curse when Kelly left him to make babies with a man who wanted them. She'd gotten drunk with him the day his divorce papers came through.

"I can't go until you tell me what's going on."

That perfectly sculpted chin lifted again.

"I'm six-and-a-half weeks pregnant."

Joe dropped his water bottle.

"I WON'T LET the business suffer."

Shocked at the emotions running through him—anger at the man who'd done this to her, feelings of protectiveness—Joe loosened his tie and sat. Darin and Samantha both leaped from the sofa and scurried out of the room.

The idea of Elise pregnant was so far removed from his idea of reality he couldn't quite get his mind around it.

"B&R didn't even enter my head."

"Well, it will, and I want you to know that I'm prepared to do whatever it takes to handle my responsibilities the same as I always have."

He didn't doubt her. And at the moment didn't care.

Looking her in the eye, he sought to explain the inexplicable. "Who's the father?" And why did he already hate the guy so much?

"I don't know."

Fire burned beneath his skin. How did a woman—at least the kind of woman Elise was—get pregnant without knowing the father? Unless she'd been raped. Could a woman go through something like that and never let on? Surely even Elise, as strong and unflappable and self-contained as she was, couldn't do that.

And how did he tackle such a sensitive and

intimate subject? He didn't want to trigger a break-down.

He thought of the times he'd seen her cry.

There weren't any.

The times she'd come to him with a personal problem.

There weren't any of those, either.

"When are you due?"

"Christmas."

He couldn't help a quick glance at her midsection. It was as flat as ever.

"I won't let you and the business down, Joe," she repeated.

"I'm not worried about me! *Or* the business." Did she think he was that shallow?

"You're obviously upset."

"I'd like to kill the bastard who did this to you."

"*I* did this to me."

Had her expression not been so earnest, the situation so tragic, he would have chuckled. "My friend, you are the most self-sufficient woman I've ever met, but even you cannot produce the necessary male ingredient for procreation."

"No, but I can buy it."

Her skirt had pink flowers on it. And dark smudges along the hem. He waited.

"I had artificial insemination."

"You meant to get pregnant?"

"Yeah."

"Good God, woman! What the hell did you do that for?"

"I want a family, Joe!" Her brows rose with her voice, giving her an air of desperation. Panic. He had no idea what to do.

"But—"

She shook her head. "Don't 'but' me right now, okay? This isn't up for debate. It's a done deal."

"I'm trying to understand."

"How could you?" Elise got up and left the room so quickly, he was pretty sure she wasn't coming back. And wished there were a door that would allow him to quietly slip away without having to pass through the inner domain of her home. He wished she had a best friend he could call to take over where he was grossly inadequate.

"Here." She was back. With a shot of bourbon mixed with water.

Joe accepted the gift without a word. Took a long sip. And stared at ice cubes floating in amber-colored liquid.

Sitting down on the other end of the couch, Elise leaned forward, her elbows on her knees, and turned her head toward him. "How many guys have I dated more than once in the last five years?"

"Two that I know of."

"Then you know of all of them."

He was treading on uncharted ground. He'd been confiding in her about his love life for most of the time he'd known her. All he knew of hers was what they'd just covered.

"You're a strikingly beautiful woman, Elise." Surely she knew that. "You could have any man you wanted."

Still she watched him. "I didn't think you ever noticed I'm a woman."

The glass started to slide through Joe's sweaty fingers. He got a better grip.

"I noticed. But you made it plain from the beginning that you valued our friendship and wanted it to stay that way."

"I did. I do."

"I respected that."

Staring at her clasped hands, she was silent for a long moment. "I have a little story to tell you."

He waited.

"One I should've told you years ago."

"Why didn't you?"

"I'm not sure," she said, frowning as she peered over at him again. "My reasons seem silly now, and yet to me they make perfect sense."

He had no idea what any of this had to do with her newly disclosed pregnancy, but knowing Elise, he was certain he was going to find out. What surprised him was how badly everything about this evening threatened him. He was generally a flexible guy. Took change on the cuff. Accepted other people and their choices, whether like his or not, without much difficulty. He'd grown up in a family with seven kids, and someone was always doing something he didn't like. To survive, he'd learned the wisdom of withholding judgment.

"You mentioned my looks just now, as though my being beautiful was just part of who I am."

"Isn't it?" Joe asked her. She used to intrigue and frustrate him with her insights. He hadn't realized she'd stopped sharing them until this moment when he realized that one was on its way. He sat back, waiting.

He'd missed them.

"No. My looks aren't me at all."

"We all have outer packaging," he countered. A philosophical debate he could do. And even if he couldn't, he was willing to try—anything to delay the moment they'd have to get back to the problem at hand. "It's a part of you, just like your gender. And your sense of humor. It shapes many of life's experiences and has no bearing on others."

"Exactly, it's a package. One we're born with. It gives us a sense of self from our earliest moments."

She didn't usually agree so quickly. "Right."

"It combines with our memories, our loved ones, to provide the rock upon which our lives are built. No matter what happens to us, we can go back to that rock and find solid ground."

"Uh-huh."

Joe watched her through narrowed eyes. There was a catch here. He could feel it coming.

"And that's why I didn't tell you my little story before now," Elise said. "I didn't want you to know I don't have that rock. You treated me like I was normal, and normal was something I hadn't felt in far too many years."

"Too many years," Joe repeated. "You sound as if you were forty when I met you." He wondered if pregnancy had already gotten to her emotions. One second she was Elise, and the next she wasn't making any sense at all. "You weren't even eighteen."

"And you treated me like it. You wouldn't have if I'd told you what I'd already endured before I got to my freshman year at the University of Michigan."

The room was warm. Joe chugged the last of his drink.

"I'm not the woman you see, Joe."

He didn't believe her.

CHAPTER TWO

ELISE WATCHED THE EMOTIONS flit across the face of her dear friend and partner. Joe had always been so easy to read. He didn't have anything to hide.

His open honesty made him a great salesman.

And a horrible poker player.

He didn't want to hear what she had to say.

But he *had* to hear it.

Maybe as badly as she now needed to quit hiding from the truth.

"This face you find strikingly beautiful…" The words caught in her throat. She'd loved hearing Joe describe her that way, but she needed to bury her head and cry at the same time. It wasn't her he was admiring.

It wasn't *ever* her.

"It's not me, Joe. It's a piece of art—the award-winning work of a very talented craftsman."

Dr. Thomas Fuller hadn't told her about the public acknowledgment of his work—or the pictures of her face that had been passed around. She'd seen a magazine open to an article in his office one day.

And had rushed to his private bathroom to throw up.

"I don't understand," Joe said.

"You know B&R's start-up money came from a life insurance policy my father purchased before he died." When it came right down to it, even after all the years of counseling, the new steps she'd vowed to take, she still couldn't find the words to speak of the night that had irrevocably changed her life forever.

"Yes." Joe twirled his glass, moving the ice cubes around and around.

"I'll get you another drink."

He didn't argue.

"I was born in Arkansas," she said as she came back into the room and handed him the full glass. She took her bottle of water to the other end of the sofa. Opened it. Played with the lid. "I was third youngest of four kids."

"You have siblings?"

She couldn't blame him for sounding so shocked. Yet the reaction cut her to the core.

And that was why she was speaking up. People couldn't know what she didn't tell them.

"A brother and two sisters."

He threw up a hand. "Why haven't I ever met them? You know all *my* brothers and sisters. Hell, you know their kids better than I do."

She'd spent a lot of holidays with his family.

And she'd hurt him. She hadn't expected that.

They're dead, Joe. The words said themselves in her head.

"You're welcome to meet my family right now if you'd like to take a five-minute drive with me to the cemetery."

"They're dead?"

She tried to nod. Meant to nod. She stared at him. Not even blinking.

"All of them?"

Now she blinked, opened her mouth, but it was trembling too badly to wrap around words.

His face stiffened, and paled. "How?"

"A fire. The electrical system in our house shorted."

JOE'S SKIN WAS CLAMMY. Chilled. He needed to walk. Do something. But he couldn't move.

Surely the horror he was beginning to picture wasn't as bad as he was seeing it. Elise was his friend—probably the best friend he'd ever had. She was strong and steady. Nothing bad ever happened to her.

How could he have been so blind? So damned self-interested that he hadn't known she was hiding?

"They didn't have time to get out?" he asked now, aghast at the thought of her siblings trapped in a burning home.

"It was the middle of the night."

The story she'd had to tell him was simple enough. But it contained images he was never going to forget. His beautiful, self-sufficient partner sitting on her sofa, hunched over, consumed by inner visions. And a fear so real she was shaking with it.

"What about your parents?"

"Them, too."

She'd lost her entire family in one tragic night. He couldn't even fathom such a thing. Not when his siblings, his parents, were still very much alive and in his life, an intrinsic part of who he was.

He stared at his friend, seeing someone completely different, someone his heart bled for. Someone he was in awe of.

"How old were you?"

She didn't seem to see him. "Eleven."

A child. An innocent. Six years before he met her. Six years of growing up…where? With whom?

"Where were you at the time?" How had she been told? Did she see the house?

"There. I was there."

Joe fought the images. He thought about holding her until it all went away.

And then the end of the story became terrifyingly clear. She'd referred to herself as the award-winning work of a talented craftsman. She wasn't who he saw.

"You were burned."

She cringed, hugged her knees. And nodded.

He watched. Waited for her to look up at him. Could he pull her into his arms and make it better? Should he touch her?

Elise's eyes, when she finally raised her head, revealed the child she'd been. She seemed unsure of his reaction—as though she'd been expecting a negative one.

He swallowed. Fought the urge to run his fingers over her face, through her hair, to kiss away the tears glistening in her lashes. To take her into his lap and rock her.

"How badly?"

"Forty percent."

Of her body? Trying to imagine the reality made him sick to his stomach. The pain would have been excruciating. Enough to send an adult over the edge, let alone an eleven-year-old child.

"Hair ignites quickly," she said now, her voice more that of a young girl than the indomitable woman he'd known. "It's highly flammable."

Joe had nothing to say. His eyes stung. He took her hand.

"Mine was long."

ELISE HAD NO IDEA HOW much time had passed. Caught in a warp between past and present, long-ago pain and current fear, she pushed words past the constriction in her throat as best she could. Spoke, for the first time to a nonmedical person, about the night a large part of her died, leaving behind the intelligent automaton who assessed life, made wise decisions, lived up to societal expectations, was kind to others—and had no sense of personal identity whatsoever.

Holding Joe's hand—another first—she answered his questions as best as she could, telling him about the years of reconstructive surgeries.

"Dr. Fuller was an angel sent from God," she told him. "I met him at the burn unit when I was first brought in, although I don't remember that." She smiled, despite the tears in her eyes. "From what I've been told, he took one look at me, heard that my family had all died in the fire, and declared himself my provider and protector. He worked with Social Services and I was placed in the home of his parents' dearest friends—when I wasn't in the hospital. I was the culmination of his life's work, and he performed operations that normally cost exorbitant amounts, at the fee covered by my insurance."

Elise, withstanding Joe's perusal with difficulty, could feel her skin tightening where she still had surface sensation. Even after all those years in and out of hospitals, she'd never gotten used to the stares—and the accompanying horror on the faces of the strangers who'd seen her.

"It's amazing there aren't any scars."

"There are." She closed her eyes, reached with her free hand to trace her hair line. "Here—" her finger moved down the outside of her jawbone to beneath her chin "—to here."

There were other scars he couldn't see. That no one saw. Both inside and out. But she was lucky. Thanks to Thomas Fuller, the only external signs left from that hateful night were skillfully hidden, mere thin, silky lines.

"And the people who kept you, they were kind?"

"Very." If she tried really hard, she could still smell Mary's peach cobbler baking in the oven. "The Bournes were a childless couple in their seventies. My parents were both estranged from their families because they'd married outside their religions—one was Jewish, one Catholic. So I never knew either set of my grandparents. The time I spent with the Bournes was a gift. Mostly I remember their kindness. They carted me back and forth to appointments, therapies and surgeries, visiting me whenever I was in the hospital."

"Where are they now?"

"Wally died of a heart attack the year before I started college. Mary followed about six months later. They were both eighty-one."

"I knew you then."

"Barely."

"You never let on you were grieving…"

Joe shook his head. It must be late. He couldn't let go of Elise's hand—as though his touch made a difference to her aloneness.

"I'm so incredibly sorry," he said, hating how trite the words sounded. He'd asked what she'd meant by therapy, and she'd told him about the years of painful treatments she'd endured to regain full use of her injured muscles and limbs. About the nerves that couldn't be fixed, the parts of her face that would never experience sensation again.

"Thanks." She didn't seem to notice that her fingers were still clasped in his. "You're the first person I've ever told about this—apart from counselors."

He frowned, wishing he'd taken more time to get to know her over the years. He had an idea he'd missed out on much. "Why is that?"

"Look at how you're looking at me."

He blinked, pulled away. Let go of her hand. "What?"

"You feel sorry for me."

"Of course I do! You suffered such a tragedy."

"I know. And I appreciate the sympathy, don't get me wrong. But after everything I'd been through, I just wanted to live a normal life. It wasn't ever going to happen if I took my past with me."

"Your past is a part of you."

She was busy trying to leave it behind. "Maybe."

"It made you strong."

She didn't feel strong.

"I've dated two wonderful men in the past five years, and both times I could never get enough sense of who I was to be able to give my heart to someone. There's always this part of me that's detached."

She figured that there was no point in holding back now. Joe already knew the worst. And he was safe. A friend and no more.

"I feel fake inside," she admitted to him. "Just like my face is fake."

She drew back when he reached to touch her, but he ran his fingers down the side of her cheek anyway. "You don't feel fake."

She didn't feel his fingers, either.

And then, as his hand continued over her face, away from the grafted skin, she did.

"I lost everything, Joe. Mementos, photos, tokens. The memories fade and there's no one left who shared them to remind me. I look in the mirror and I'm not me. There is nothing there that speaks of my heritage."

He started to speak but she held up a hand. She had to finish what she'd started.

"Don't get me wrong. I'm not feeling sorry for myself here," she continued. "Yes, horrible things happened, but I was also incredibly lucky—in many ways—and I'm very grateful for that. Truthfully, I think more about the good than the bad."

He nodded, sipped his watered-down drink, then held the glass in both hands in his lap.

"I'm a survivor, Joe. I'm only telling you about all this so that you can understand."

And because, as of today, there was no way her choice wasn't going to affect his life, as well, at least peripherally.

"I'm thirty-two years old. I've got my body back, my career and financial security are set, but my sense of self, of being grounded, which I lost in that fire, is still missing. I have no significant other. I've been finding my solutions on my own for a long time."

"And so you decided to have a baby, start a new family, on your own."

The knot between her shoulder blades loosened and Elise almost smiled. "Yes." He got it.

"Okay." He drained his drink, sat forward. "You have my full support."

Elise was tempted to stand, to leave it at that and let him leave, but knew she couldn't. She'd opened the door to truth between them. She was no longer hiding.

"There's more, Joe."

Lips pursed, he nodded. "I kind of thought so."

"I had an ultrasound today."

He peered at her through narrowed eyes. "There's something wrong with the baby?"

If she didn't know better, she'd think he was personally invested in her answer. But this was Joe. He'd chosen divorce over creating a baby with the woman he adored.

"Not as far as they can tell," she answered slowly.

"So what's the problem?"

"There are four of them."

JOE DROVE HOME. His older brother Kenny was waiting on the lighted basketball court behind Joe's home, just as Joe had requested from his cell phone immediately after leaving Elise.

Kenny, like Joe, was unmarried, unencumbered with a houseful of needs that couldn't possibly be met. He was also unemployed—for the fourth time in almost as many years.

By choice.

His brother got bored easily.

"What's up?" Kenny asked as Joe joined him five minutes later, having exchanged his shirt and tie for shorts, a T-shirt and three-hundred-dollar tennis shoes.

"Just needed a game," Joe grunted as he sank a three-pointer.

Kenny swiveled, butted up against Joe as he dribbled and went up for a successful slam dunk. "It's after nine o'clock. You work in the morning."

"*You* don't, so what's it to you?" Joe rebounded, took the ball back and lined up another three.

With a quick jump, Kenny stole the ball from him.

"As a matter of fact, I do," Kenny said, turning to grin at Joe as he bounced the ball between his legs and caught it behind him. "I sold Wambo."

One of Kenny's many animated video characters. He named a well-known, international video game producer as the buyer.

"I've got some changes to make to him—he needs to be a little taller and more agile. And they want a woman to go with him."

Joe stood while Kenny made the next shot. His brother was up on him four to three. "Congratulations!" he said, slapping Kenny on the back.

Kenny got his own rebound and shot the ball at Joe's chest.

"Can't let you be the richest guy in the family," he joked, but Joe could tell that his big brother was proud of Joe's accomplishments, too. Mostly Joe was relieved to see that Kenny was finally finding some success with what he most loved to do. What he was good at.

He deserved it.

Joe sank another three. And was in his brother's face, up and down the half court, pounding the pavement, the backboard, anything he came in contact with as he trounced one of Michigan State's most celebrated basketball stars.

Kenny asked him again what was wrong.

Joe insisted nothing was wrong. And he showered and went to bed telling himself the same thing.

Elise was a business partner who'd survived incredible odds.

Her private life was not and never had been any concern of his.

Sleep was elusive.

ELEVEN O'CLOCK and Elise still couldn't quiet her mind at all. She'd taken a hot bath. Done breathing exercises. She'd watched a sitcom. Tried to read—and to coax her independent housemates out from under the bed.

And then she picked up the phone. It was an hour earlier in Arkansas. He'd be home by now after his evening jog. Turning seventy hadn't slowed him down a bit.

"Elise! Good to hear from you."

Standing in the middle of her bedroom, Elise studied herself in the antique free-standing, floor-length mirror. There wasn't a single visible scar on her face. And her body was almost as beautiful.

"I'm sorry to bother you so late."

"You are never a bother, my dear. But I hear something in your voice that concerns me. Need to talk?"

He'd know it was why she'd called. Why, after all the years since being his patient, she still called. At least once a month. She'd grown up with Thomas, confided her deepest secrets to him, trusted his advice.

After the death of her family, he'd become her protector.

There'd been a time of despair—of separation—when he'd fallen from his pedestal. He'd published photos of her at the various stages of her plastic surgery. She'd long since forgiven him, though.

Now he was just a man. And a very dear friend, with faults and failings like everyone else.

And he'd created the woman who now stood on expensive carpet in a spacious bedroom in a beautiful old home in Lowell, Michigan.

"I'm pregnant, Thomas."

"Congratulations!" her ex-doctor said with real joy. "So it took the first time!"

"It more than took." She turned away from her

image as fear twisted her features. "I'm carrying quadruplets."

He swore—something he rarely did. And that scared her anew.

"You're worried," she said.

"No," he answered immediately, his voice reassuring even halfway across the nation. "Just wishing that something would come easy for you."

"Yeah, me, too."

Silence. He had doubts. She'd known he would. Feared he would.

Sinking to the handmade floral quilt on her king-size bed, she asked, "What am I going to do, Thomas?"

"Follow doctor's orders explicitly and have healthy babies."

The answer surprised her.

"And after that?"

"You'll raise them."

"How?" She only had two arms.

"You lived through six years of agonizing pain and debilitation, Elise, beating all the odds over and over again. And you did most of it with a smile on your face. What's raising four children after that?"

Four children was one thing. Four children *at once* was another.

"They talked about selective reduction."

"It's an option."

"What do you think?"

"Removing one or two fetuses is common

enough practice in quadruplet pregnancies. But it also poses risks to the remaining fetus or fetuses."

"Do you think I should do it?"

"Do you want to?"

No. Not at all. She could hardly bear the thought. But for the sake of doing the right thing, she was forcing herself to consider the option.

"You can do this," he said. "You can go through this pregnancy, have these babies, do a good job raising them."

"I'm scared to death."

"It's not the first time, is it?"

He knew it wasn't.

"Hey." His voice came again, softer now. "Have you forgotten the one rule of life?"

His wife, Elizabeth, had taught it to her. And to emphasize the message, after every single procedure Elise had undergone during the six years of her recovery, there'd been a gift waiting for her when she awoke.

"To always look for the gift in every situation," she repeated now.

"You wanted a family. You're thirty-two. By the time you're thirty-three, you'll have a full house."

With a trembling chin, Elise faced the mirror again. "Mama raised four babies. So can I."

"That's my girl."

CHAPTER THREE

JOE DIDN'T GET ANGRY OFTEN.

Anger brought chaos, for which Joe had a deep-seated aversion.

He avoided glances from everyone in the payroll department as he strode the short distance from his office on one end of the fifteenth-floor condominium suite to Elise's office on the other.

It had been two weeks and a day since he'd met the real Elise Richardson—or at least a more complete Elise.

Two weeks and a day since she'd told him she was carrying four babies at once.

Neither of them had mentioned the conversation since.

He could think of little else.

She was on the phone when he arrived. The second she disconnected he announced, "I just heard you climbed fifteen flights of stairs with a bag of groceries."

He could only see the top half of her sleeveless white summer dress, and she wasn't sweating a bit.

"I had salad dressing and meat for the chicken Caesar salad we're having for lunch. I couldn't leave them in my car. It's summer outside, in case you haven't noticed."

"Don't humor me, Elise. I'm not out of line here."

"You're upset over nothing." She didn't have to flick her fingers through that short dark hair to make her opinion perfectly clear.

"You climbed fifteen flights of stairs!"

"The elevator was out."

"You're carrying four babies! You should have called someone."

She glanced to the hall outside the big glass windows on either side of her door. "The bag wasn't heavy and exercise is good." Her voice had lost much of its force.

"You still haven't told anyone."

She shook her head.

"When are you planning to do it?"

"As soon as the timing's right. At the moment we're hiring a new pay tech to take care of the payroll-only clients. And something's up with one of our couriers—checks have been misdelivered twice."

"Lunch today would be good timing," Joe said, refusing to be distracted by business when what he really wanted was to never again speak of anything else with his partner. "Putting yourself—and your babies—in danger is ludicrous."

"There was no danger, Joe! I'm not stupid. I

went slowly, took breaks when I needed to. I just saw my doctor this morning and she says the more I exercise the better we're all going to be."

He closed her door, then stood in front of her desk like some kind of drill sergeant. Unusual for him.

"On to something that matters," she said, eyeing him with warning. "First International is threatening to raise our group rate again. I've got an appointment on Monday with Great State."

Both substantial and reputable insurance companies, and nothing to do with the stairs she'd climbed—or the reason he cared that she had. "I suspect their quotes will be similar."

"Our value comes in offering insurance to employees of independent companies at a rate their companies can't afford to offer. If our rates change too much, we lose that value."

"We offer a great package," he said. "Payroll, workers' comp, tax compliance—*and* group insurance. And if our rates raise, so will everyone else's. Unless they drop the lower rate structure for larger groups—which would put them out of business— we'll still have the advantage."

"I have an idea that will give us more of an advantage."

He recognized the glint in her eye and sat in a visitor chair. "I'm listening."

"What if we bundle a package of vendors? You know, a workers' comp specialist, a strategic planning counselor, a tax consultant, a retirement counselor, psychiatric counselor, a corporate lawyer and maybe some kind of team facilitator—all things that are offered to employees of larger companies."

"Benefits that bring higher levels of success," he added, already hearing the presentation in his mind as he imagined himself selling the idea.

"Exactly." Elise folded her hands on her desk, watching him. "The vendors would all bill us and we'd bill the companies, based on how many options they choose."

"Individual services billed at a package-deal rate."

"Correct."

He loved it. Would have thought of it himself if he didn't have her there to do that kind of thinking for him. Or not.

The tension that had become almost a constant companion to Joe these past couple of weeks returned in force. He needed Elise. Couldn't afford to lose her. B&R couldn't afford to lose her.

But how could four newborn babies possibly fit into the mix? Or four toddlers, for that matter?

"SO WHAT ELSE DID the doctor say?"

Elise stared at Joe, at the closed door to her office, then the hallway. They were working. In ten years, they'd never talked about personal stuff during working hours. At least not *her* personal stuff. She wasn't forthcoming. He never asked. This was the second time in an hour.

She didn't want that to change. Maybe she'd

made a horrible mistake—or many of them. Confiding in Joe about her past. And her present. Visiting the fertility clinic. Thinking she needed more out of life. Thinking, period.

"You know doctors," she conceded with an answer of sorts when it became clear that he'd sit there through the noon hour if she didn't ante up. "They're always worried about malpractice suits."

Sitting forward, Joe held her gaze, not bothering to temper his frown with even a hint of a smile. "What did she say?"

Angela Parks walked by—probably on her way to the water fountain, judging by the big blue thermal cup in her hand. She filled it at least three times a day. Elise was a little concerned that the twenty-five-year-old pay tech might be diabetic.

"She went over the potential risks." She'd also given Elise a written list of them. She needn't have bothered. They were stamped so clearly on her mind she was having trouble focusing on other things.

"Such as?"

Joe looked so earnest, sitting there, his tie slightly askew. Should she tell him? Didn't he see they were pushing boundaries here? Was he ready for that?

Was *she?*

"Premature birth is the biggest. A normal pregnancy goes forty weeks. If mine goes to thirty-four she'll be pleased. Thirty-one is average."

"Does she see any reason you won't?"

"No. Not at all."

"What else?"

"Even if I make it to thirty-*six* weeks, the babies will have lower than normal birth weights."

"Why is that?"

"With four of them sharing space, their growing room is limited."

He fidgeted in his seat, looked down.

"Anything more?" he asked, taking a noticeable degree of interest in a speck on his shoe.

She threw out a hand, wishing she felt even a tenth as nonchalant as she'd have him believe. "Various little problems I'll be prone to with that many babies pressing on my internal organs."

Elise started to sweat again, just thinking about the "little problems" of gestational hypertension, anemia, diabetes or any of the other things Dr. Braden had warned her about. She'd never considered, until that morning, that she wouldn't be physically capable of taking care of herself through all this. She was strong. A survivor.

And if she didn't, who would?

Helplessness was not an option for family-less people.

"I'm assuming she had orders for you?"

Dozens of them. A few she'd share. "Just lots of rest, a careful diet and vitamins at this point," she told him honestly. She couldn't think about any more than that. Being confined to bed the last trimester wasn't an option.

Elise's life was about miracles. She'd survived the fire that had killed her entire family. She had little trace of the burns that had covered forty percent of her body. She could be one of the three percent of women who had relatively normal quadruplet pregnancies—and she'd start the percentage for those who made it the entire way upright.

"Did she advise you to quit work?"

"No." Not yet, anyway. Dr. Braden expected she'd eventually prescribe bed rest, though. She probably assumed that Elise would understand that bed rest meant not working.

The assumption was wrong.

"MAY I HAVE YOUR ATTENTION please?"

Joe stood in the doorway of the kitchen, searching the room for his partner. She was over by the sink, still serving plates of food.

When she'd originally started the tradition of providing Friday lunch, their office had been one room with partitions and she'd cooked at home and brought lunch in. There'd been just the two of them and they'd pulled up chairs at Joe's desk and eaten together.

Voices slowly stopped as faces turned toward him. Joe counted all nine of them. Everyone was there. Good.

"Sorry to interrupt your lunch, but we have an announcement to make. Elise?"

He would not feel guilty about this. Elise's health was at risk.

"Ah, yes." He heard her voice and studied the flooring. The travertine had been a good choice. Elise's, of course.

"B&R is going to expand our program of services…"

What? He did everything he could to bore a hole with his eyes into his partner's forehead as she expounded on the plan the two of them had agreed upon that morning, giving their employees assignments, timelines and a bonus program. The woman was good.

But she wasn't getting away with it.

After the applause died down and questions were answered, Joe stepped farther into the room.

"That isn't all Elise has to say," he told the group. This time his gaze let her know in no uncertain terms that if she didn't do this, he would.

She'd put away the lunch leftovers and moved aside as Ruth Gregory and the two girls who worked under her supervision carried over the dishes and started rinsing them.

"I…"

Her eyes pleaded with him. He didn't back down.

"I…"

"You aren't quitting, are you?" The horrified call came from the end of the room. Sam Watterson, his senior sales associate.

"No!" Elise's eyes met Joe's again, and he finally understood. She wasn't trying to be difficult. She wasn't even trying to be secretive.

She just couldn't do this.

"What Elise is trying to tell you is that she's going to need your help a little bit more than usual around here over the next few months. We all know how much she's given to this company—to all of us—and now it's time for us to thank her by returning the support. Starting with congratulations. She's decided to start a family."

Exclamations broke out around them, heads jerking toward Elise, as though for confirmation that Joe was sane and not telling stories about her.

"Yes, yes, it's true," she said. She stood in the center of the room as though uncertain of how to respond to the smiling faces around her.

"Are you going to adopt a boy or a girl?" Ruth asked.

Elise's expression froze. "Uh…"

"She's not adopting," Joe jumped in, cursing himself. It wasn't like him to act without foresight, without planning. But then, it wasn't like his partner to get pregnant, either.

"You're going to have a baby?" Angela's voice rose with excitement. She was at Elise's right elbow.

Elise nodded. "More than one, actually."

"Twins?" Carolyn Ramsey, B&R's workers' compensation specialist, joined the women by the sink.

"Quadruplets," Elise said as though it was commonplace. The woman just wasn't facing the situation, Joe thought. Which worried the hell out of him. How could he count on her to take care of herself if she wasn't going to acknowledge what needed to be done?

Whatever the hell that was.

Everyone in the room was staring. "I'm eight-and-a-half weeks along," Elise added.

"Quadruplets!" Angela's eyes were wide. "Cool. I've never known anyone who had four kids at once."

"Are you going to tell us next that you're the happy father?" Mark Oppenheimer asked, taking his plate to the sink.

The idea floored Joe.

But not, apparently, their staff. The room grew quiet, eyes on him.

"No, he's not," Elise said at last. "Joe's a wonderful business partner, but spare me his eating habits. I could never live with a man who eats leftover pizza for breakfast."

Laugher broke out and Joe started to breathe again. She'd never experienced the bliss of cold pizza in the morning? That was her problem.

"Nor could I expose my children to such habits with a clear conscience," she continued.

"Then who…"

"But…"

He should have anticipated the awkward situation he'd put her·in. Should have done this differently. Presentation was his business.

"Elise elected to do this alone," he told the

group. "She had artificial insemination, and I, for one, admire the hell out of her for having the courage to pursue her own brand of happiness."

Cheers filled the room and Joe could no longer make out the excited chatter around Elise. He waited around another minute or two—long enough to make sure that she was okay, and then escaped to his office.

She'd be well taken care of. If he'd read their staff right—and reading people, Elise aside, was one of his most prominent skills—she'd have no fewer than nine surrogate watchdogs at the office over the next months.

Which let him solidly off the hook.

"HI, ELIZABETH, it's Elise. Is Thomas home?"

Seven-thirty on Saturday morning, he should be. Unless he had a golf game. Samantha rubbed up against her, purring.

"Of course. Let me get him for you, dear."

"Thanks."

"I hear congratulations are in order. I was thrilled when Thomas told me it worked so quickly. And don't worry about the rest of it, dear. You know how the good Lord works. In his time, not yours. He's taken pretty good care of you."

Including sending such a wise woman to keep her head straight, Elise thought. If only she had Elizabeth's confidence. "I know."

"I'll get Thomas."

"ARE YOU FEELING OKAY?" Thomas's greeting was right to the point as always when he came on the line moments later.

"Yes."

"Following doctor's orders?"

"Don't I always?"

"Any problems?"

"Not so far."

"Good. So you like this Dr. Braden? You trust her?"

"Uh-huh."

"I made some calls—heard nothing but good about her."

Elise smiled, though she almost started to cry, as well. "Am I ever going to get too old for you to look out for me?"

"Nope."

She was glad to hear that.

"It's going to be hard carrying four babies at once."

"Harder on some than others. You're strong and in excellent health. Just keep taking all your vitamins."

She paused, knowing what he'd say, but she had to voice her concerns anyway. If not, they'd continue to go around in her head driving her quietly insane.

"What if something happens to me, Thomas? What'll happen to my children?" Darin jumped into her lap and she stroked his back.

"You trying to do God's job again?"

Just as she'd expected.

"No."

"Lots of things can happen. Each with its own solution based on where you are in life when it happens. No point trying to find solutions for circumstances that are not yet set."

Also what she'd expected.

"Then can we deal with here and now?" she asked. "I'm afraid there are a million things I'm not thinking of."

"I doubt that, my dear, but I'm happy to help, you know that. Tell me what you've done to provide for the kids in case something happens to you."

"I took out another life insurance policy last week." Her father had taught her well.

"Good. Anything else?"

"Set up a trust."

"Excellent."

"Will you and Elizabeth execute for me?"

"For now."

In a routine established years before, he helped her organize her thoughts one by one. Breaking everything down into parts she could manage.

"I've got all this energy," she told him half an hour later. "I'm supposed to be tired, aren't I?"

"Wait another couple of weeks," he replied. "In the meantime, why not shop? You're going to need four of everything. Make your choices, have things delivered, get the house ready in case you're too tired to walk from one room to another later on."

Four cribs. Where was she going to put them?

She moved through the house. The family room would need cradles. And a changing table. And swings. Nothing in the living room.

Four of everything. The cribs would all fit in the second bedroom.

Too tired to walk, he'd said. Oh, God. Could she do this?

"Do you recommend disposable diapers?" Thomas was still on the phone. She had to say something.

"For a single mother of four? Absolutely! Get on the Internet, Elise, and find one of those quad scooter things, too. They use them in place of strollers. I've seen them at conventions a time or two and I'm guessing you won't find one at a local baby store."

"Okay." And if she found one, would she have the strength to push it?

"And start looking around for a nanny now. I'm assuming you're set enough to be able to afford one?"

"During the day." She was an accountant. She'd done the math every way there was to do it. Over and over these past weeks. "We just bought the suite of offices and I owe a chunk on this house and would take huge penalties to get out of either loan."

"And knowing you, I'd guess most of your savings are tied up in long-term investments."

"IRAs, mostly. I have enough cash to see me through several months in case of an emergency, but I'll need that cushion now more than ever. I was expecting one baby. Paid maternity leave. And day care. I could do that on my salary."

"Check out programs at the local college. I think Grand Valley State is there. See if there's a child care class that will accept you as part the class curriculum. Students could get credit for assisting you with the babies while they're still too young for day care. It won't do much for your nighttime feedings, but it could sure help in the daytime at little or no cost to you. At least at the beginning. The college would screen and oversee applicants so you'd be safer than hiring someone on your own."

Elise sat down on the queen-size bed in her second guest room, smiling and crying at the same time. "You are a godsend, my friend."

"I'm an old man. Live long enough and you hear about everything."

"I'll call the college on Monday. Thanks for the idea."

They chatted another twenty minutes or so, and when she hung up, Elise's smile was genuine.

Thomas could always instill the sense that she wasn't alone even when she was.

CHAPTER FOUR

SATURDAY MORNINGS were sacred. Free time to do whatever he wanted. The time reserved for no responsibility. The complete antithesis to the Saturdays of Joe's youth that began before the sun rose with a house full of arguing and whining and the unending chores that the conglomeration of needs and wants of so many children living under one roof necessitated.

He was thinking about taking his canoe out to the river, seeing how far he could get before stopping at one of the restaurants on the shore for lunch. Some were right at the mouth of the Flat River, where it joined the Grand River, but he could travel seventy miles on the Flat alone if he wanted to. Of course his favorite little diner was right there on Main Street in Lowell.

Maybe he'd go to the gym and shoot some hoops instead. And then go to the Levee for lunch. If he went to the gym he'd have to shower again.

Turning off Main Street along the river, Joe considered the canoe again. A day alone, and the physical exertion of paddling sounded good. He could pack a lunch and spend the whole day on the water. The sun was shining, not a cloud in the sky. The July temperatures were perfect. And there would be a breeze on the river.

Sounded like heaven.

He passed her house. Continued on.

She'd taken off after making tacos for them all for lunch yesterday. She'd had her twelve-week doctor's appointment.

Joe slowed. Turned around. He had to go back for his canoe anyway. And to exchange his sandals for running shoes and put sunscreen on skin left exposed by his denim shorts and loose tank top. He should probably grab a T-shirt instead. Right after he stopped by Elise's. He'd hoped she'd call—not that she ever had before—but he had an investment in what was going on here. His livelihood was firmly tied to hers. If something happened to her...

Joe pulled into her drive.

SOMEONE WAS AT the front door. Staring at the bathroom ceiling, arms and hands lying beside her on the cool tile, Elise considered rolling over, getting up onto her hands and knees, crawling to the door. And couldn't think of a single person who would be there who would be worth the effort. A blessing, at the moment, of being alone in the world.

Her eyes were closed when the second knock came.

She was throwing up again at the third.

And by the time the side doorbell rang, she was experiencing enough of a reprieve to stand. Shakily, but at least she was upright.

The way she planned to be for the entire pregnancy, though how on earth she was going to make it through the whale stage on her feet she didn't know. She was only at the beginning of the fourth month and needed nothing as badly as she did to lie down.

After rinsing her mouth and gargling only the tiny bit of mouthwash she dared put in her mouth lest it incite another bout of retching, she shuffled her way to the door facing the river. She hadn't showered yet. Hadn't even run her fingers through her hair. And was still wearing the sweatpants and sleeveless top she'd slept in.

Samantha and Darin were entrenched firmly beneath her bed. They'd hated her retching, too.

Maybe the crib sheets had arrived. The mattresses had been bare for almost a week. Or it could be the...

"Joe?" Elise squinted up at her business partner, feeling as though she'd stepped onto another planet. Joe played on Saturday mornings. She'd never once heard from him then. Not even in college.

"I thought you were a changing table," she said, leaning against the door, half blinded by sunlight. "I was hoping to get it put together this weekend," she added irrelevantly.

He'd never seen her without makeup. She felt too wretched to care.

"I got you out of bed."

"No." She started to shake her head and stopped. Too much movement, too quickly. "I've been up over an hour."

Making love to the toilet.

"What's wrong?" Something had to be or he wouldn't be there. And whatever it was, she'd deal with it. She'd promised him.

"That's what I'm about to ask you."

"Oh. I'm fine." She leaned her head against the door. "Just trying to convince my children that eating is a necessary part of my life."

She'd started laughing at herself half an hour before. Right after sobbing had caused another bout of vomiting.

He frowned, staring at her.

"Morning sickness," she explained and bit back a smile at the embarrassed dawning of understanding that crossed his features.

"Should I call a doctor?"

"Nope. It's happened before. It'll pass. I could be as good as new in a matter of minutes."

He shifted his weight from one foot to the other. "It looks to me like you should spend the day in bed. If it's anything like the flu, you need rest to regain your energy."

"Nope. Eating takes care of that—once I'm allowed to do so."

"Is it always this bad?"

She really wasn't in the mood to chat.

"For me, or in general?"

"Either."

"For me, yes. In general, I have no idea. But I'd guess not. I can't imagine women electing to go through this a second time."

He had to have a reason for being there other than the state of her stomach. It would be good if he'd just tell her and be on his way before she gave in to the urge to slide down to lie on the floor. The entryway was tile, too, and tile was her friend. It was cool. And didn't move at all.

He didn't say anything. Didn't seem to be leaving.

"My theory is that if one kid objects to nutrition, all the rest will decide to give it a try."

She'd come up with this theory in the middle of the night a week or so ago, picturing her four offspring with minds and motivations of their own—it made them seem more endurable somehow.

Joe's bark of laughter surprised her. She wasn't usually able to amuse him.

"They're considerate brats, though," she continued babbling, closing her eyes as she felt the breeze coming up from the river across the street. "They refrain from midday or evening interruptions, keeping all food rejections to the night and first thing in the morning."

Would he never leave? The living room sofa was

through the foyer door and six yards away. The light green cushions were silky, soft. They'd be cool.

And they didn't smell.

She could let go of the door. Take enough steps to make it there.

The world would stop spinning as soon as she lay down. In another fifteen minutes, assuming her babies were done protesting, she'd be good to go.

Cool cushions against her cheek. Six yards away. Fifteen minutes.

Pushing off from the open door, Elise stumbled toward her destination.

JOE CRACKED HIS ARM against the doorjamb in his haste, but he got to her before she hit the floor. With fear in his heart, he picked up his partner, holding her gingerly as he carried her to the closest piece of furniture in the house—the living room sofa.

He'd never held her before. Wasn't even sure if they'd ever hugged as good friends sometimes do.

"Sorry," she mumbled, squinting up at him as he straightened her legs against the cushions and grabbed a throw pillow for beneath her head. "I got dizzy there for a second."

She licked lips that looked chapped. He debated calling an ambulance.

And he settled for her doctor.

"Where's your doctor's number?" he asked, striding over to the phone.

"I don't need her." Her voice sounded stronger.

Hands on his hips, Joe stared at her. "Well, you clearly need *something*. What can I do?"

"A bottle of water from the fridge might help," she said. And then, when he was halfway to the kitchen, added, "And, Joe? There's a box of crackers on the second shelf in the pantry by the stove. Would you mind bringing it, too?"

He'd have felt better calling a doctor.

TWENTY MINUTES LATER JOE conceded that she'd been right. While Elise still needed a shower and fresh clothes, her color—and her wits—were back to normal as she sat curled on one end of the couch, still munching away. She'd finished half of one of the four packs in the box he'd brought in since they'd been sitting there.

"How long has it been since you've eaten?" he finally asked, half-amused as he sat across from her. Another minute and he'd go.

"Last night." She pulled one last cracker out of the tube and put the rest in the box. "But apparently the kids don't like spinach and salmon. I don't think they let me keep any of it."

That couldn't be healthy.

Nor could walking around ready to pass out at any moment.

"Does your doctor know you live alone?"

"No."

He'd expected an affirmative. Expected to find

that there was some practical explanation for why she should be safe, alone, in her condition. He'd expected to be told that he was overreacting again.

"She thinks you have a roommate?" She'd know the history of Elise's pregnancy, surely, that she was a single woman who'd chosen artificial insemination as a means of procreating.

"Or a live-in caregiver."

The hesitant way she spoke gave him pause. And with years of practice of communicating with Elise, if not reading her expressions, he filled in the blanks.

"She told you it wasn't safe for you to be here alone."

"She said it wasn't wise."

Damn. Joe lost all appetite for a picnic lunch on the water.

"Not so much because of the morning sickness," Elise continued as he barely bit back the reprimand he needed to utter. "With four babies there's the possibility of some complications—I told you this before."

"Yeah," he muttered. What could possibly have driven her to do this to herself? Remembering that night more than a month ago when he'd met his longtime friend for the first time, he answered his own silent question.

"That's not to say there'll be any," she added quickly. "I could have a perfectly normal pregnancy."

"What are the odds?"

She hesitated.

"Of a perfectly normal pregnancy?"

He nodded.

"Three percent."

"Three percent?" Joe jumped to his feet and glared down at her—until he realized what he was doing. He sat down again, this time beside her on the sofa, and studied the class ring he'd worn since college.

"Did she tell you this yesterday?" he asked more calmly, though inside he was still bouncing off the walls.

He wasn't going to lose her over this. Couldn't she see that their lives were irreversibly linked?

Elise peered at him as though assessing his emotional weather. "Two weeks ago," she finally said quietly.

This wasn't like her. Not at all. Elise faced challenges head on. She always had a plan. She never procrastinated.

"Were you planning to wait until you had a 'complication' before you did something about having a live-in caregiver?" he asked. He instantly regretted his sarcasm. She was an adult with a right to whatever life she wanted.

His role was to support that just as she'd supported him all these years. Somehow.

"I've been reviewing potential applicants for ten days."

Joe felt relieved. "And?"

"I can't afford anyone without a police

record." She chuckled as she spoke. Joe failed to see the humor.

"The down payment on the office suite put you in a tight spot, didn't it?"

"That and the mortgage on this place," she admitted. "A couple of years ago I tied up most of my funds in an IRA. I'd lose half of it to penalties if I cash in early."

A couple of years ago they'd seen their first sizable profits in the company. He'd invested a chunk, as well. "If you'd told me that buying the suite would be a hardship we would have held off."

"Look, I'm perfectly comfortable as long as I don't see a huge increase in monthly expenses. Besides, we needed to move if we were going to continue to grow. Not only was there not enough space in the old offices for more staff, but with the kind of clients you're bringing us, these millionaire business owners, we needed an office that would instill confidence."

They'd had several conversations to that effect, he knew, mostly at her instigation. They'd both taken a risk, expecting a payoff within the next eighteen months.

"I could sell this place." She glanced around, her eyes wide and unexpectedly childlike, but when she looked at him again she was her usual practical, calm self. "But not in time to hire someone immediately. I'd have to list, sell, close and move. And in another five months or so, I'm going to need the room. Anyway," she added, her chin lifting, "I can afford this house. I make enough to provide everything I'm going to need for the babies. I just can't afford a full-time nanny. Or a full-time companion for myself while I'm pregnant."

She'd been expecting one child, not four. A normal pregnancy, not one that was going to tax her body to the limit—and possibly beyond.

"What about someone from the office? They all love you. Have you asked if anyone wants to move in here—just until the babies are born and you've got a routine established?"

"Would you want one of your employees living with you? Hearing you puke by night and taking orders from you by day?"

The sarcasm wasn't like her.

"No."

"Besides the obvious conflict of interest, there is no one." Her tone softened. "Mark and Sam are out."

"But Angela and Tamara are both single."

"You need to spend more time in the office, Joe, if you want to keep up on the staff's personal lives." Her chiding was playful. "Angela just moved in with Richard last weekend, and Tamara's mother fell and broke her hip—she's staying with Tamara indefinitely."

Joe got up and crossed to the window looking out on the sizable expanse of thick green grass that ran from house to road. He could see three huge old trees surrounded with colorfully blooming flower beds and knew there were more around back. The lot Elise's house sat on took up a city block. There were no sidewalks, just lush green space with quiet streets bordering three sides.

A perfect yard for growing kids. They could have a softball game on one side of the house, play regulation croquet, play hide-and-seek, swing as high as the sky. So why did he feel, as he stood there, that the place was a trap, imprisoning him?

His car was there—at the end of her drive. He could leave any time. Would be leaving soon for a day on the river.

He was a free man.

"*I'll* do it," he said.

FOR ONE SECOND Elise felt enormous relief. She'd never considered such a solution and it was so perfect, so right. This was about money and Joe had as much interest in her financial status as she did.

To a point.

And then he turned around. A man with a great body, wearing an old pair of denim shorts and white tank top. A man who oozed sexuality. And he was her business partner.

"It would never work," she said.

"Of course it would." His face was serious, his hands were shoved in his pockets and his feet were planted slightly apart. "It's the obvious answer."

Elise suddenly wished that she'd showered, put on makeup. Washed her hair.

She wanted to stand, too. Face him eye to eye. Knew it was important. But she couldn't do it. Not in old sweats and a sleeveless pajama top. She settled for sitting upright with her feet on the floor. Then, crossing her arms, she reminded herself that she was alone, free, boss of this house. Of her life.

"You and I are so good together because we've always managed to keep our private lives separate from our work partnership."

Not entirely true, she knew, but close enough. His expression didn't change.

"Can you imagine what we'd do to each other if we attempted to share living quarters?" she asked.

"Isn't that what we do every day?" he countered. He stepped closer. "For the past ten years we've been together at the office for more waking hours of the day than we'd be home together at night."

"But that's because we were working. And you were out on sales calls a lot."

"We co-own the office, Elise. We've managed to decorate, furnish, coexist without ever arguing."

"We argue all the time."

"We debate. And not about the office. Not about anything that matters."

That was true. But—

"Let's not make a major event out of this,

okay?" he said. Not since his mother had been diagnosed with kidney disease had he looked this serious. "It'll only be for a few months—until the babies are born and you've got a routine established. You can bring people in to help with feedings. At the end of the year, assuming I do my job, there should be enough of a profit bonus to enable you to hire a full-time nanny until the kids are old enough to go to day care. If that's what you plan."

Elise was impressed that he'd thought her life through with such detail. Still…

"No. I won't risk our working relationship because I made a choice that had unexpected consequences."

"It'll be more of a risk if B&R loses you." He was really worried that might happen.

"I told you, I won't let this affect—"

"Cut the crap, Elise," Joe said, his face flushed. "When are you going to get it? You aren't in control here. You have no way of knowing what the next months are going to bring. And if you don't start facing reality, the results could be a lot worse than they need to be."

She released a breath. "I won't let you down," she told him, every word filled with conviction. "That I know for certain, Joe. You're as much a part of my life as my arms and legs. Without you— without B&R—I have nothing. B&R gets me up in the morning. It gives me confidence and security. It challenges me. It consists of most of the people I know well in this world. I won't lose it."

"Then face facts," Joe said. "You're taking a huge risk being here alone. And I have absolutely nothing at my condo that won't do just fine without me for the next several months."

That was an understatement. She'd bought him a kitten once—he gave it to one of his sisters. She and everyone in the office had bought him a fish tank for Christmas the following year. He'd let Kelly take it in the divorce. She'd bought him plants—he'd left them at the office for her to water.

"I know your habits," he continued. "And that's half the battle of living with someone. You're an early riser, you don't stay up past eleven and you hate having the news on right before bedtime."

Elise's surprise must have shown on her face because he said, "You're at work before the cleaning crew. If I call you past eleven you're asleep and one time when Kelly and I were over for dinner, the two of you talked about watching the shopping network at night because it put you to sleep."

Elise remembered Kelly had started the conversation by enlisting her help in a battle for the bedroom TV, claiming that Joe insisted on having the news on but always fell asleep as soon as it started, leaving her to lie there in the dark and hear all kinds of horrid things.

"You don't like pizza for breakfast," he said with a completely straight face. "You eat frozen dinners, but prefer salad, and you'd rather stay in than go out at night."

Not really. But when you were a woman alone…

"It would make most sense if we eat together when we're both here," he said now. "We could share grocery costs, cooking and cleanup. But if you'd rather not, I'm okay with that, too."

"No, that's fine," she said, slightly woozy again as she filled in the pause he'd left.

"I'll pay half the utilities. Personal incidentals we'll buy separately."

"Right."

"If you show me which room I'll be using, I'll go home and pack and get moved in by tonight."

He really meant to do this.

"Joe." She reached out and grabbed the material of his shorts as he turned to head for the formal dining room and the short hall off from there that led to two of the three bedrooms. The third, hers, was directly off the dining room. "We can't do this. You can't move in here."

"I already have," he said. "I just haven't brought my stuff over yet. Now which room would you like me to use?"

It was impossible to argue with Joe when he was like this—especially when she was coming off an entire night of nausea and vomiting. At the moment, he made a doom-impending sort of sense.

He made it to the hallway before she did and had already figured out which of the two extra bedrooms he'd use. The largest had four sandalwood cribs and two white, pink and blue dressers. Darin was sleeping on top of one of the dressers. Samantha was nowhere in sight.

"I'll switch with you," Elise blurted, coming into the smaller room behind him. "Once the babies come, if you're still here, I'll need to be next to them."

He looked as if he was going to argue that, too.

"Plus, I'll be closer to the bathroom."

One of the few downsides to owning the older home. She and Joe were going to be sharing the one bathroom.

And, she was afraid, much, much more than that.

CHAPTER FIVE

JOE INTENDED TO BRING one suitcase—a couple of changes of clothes, some toiletries, shorts to sleep in. It wasn't as if he was leaving town or wouldn't have access to his condo every single day. The cell phone charger on his nightstand reminded him that he'd need it to charge the technological wonder every night while he slept so it would be up and running by morning. And there was the book next to it, the one he'd been reading each night for the past week. He was almost through with it and so added it, along with the next in the stack, to the to-go pile on his bed.

Back and forth to the bathroom a time or two and he'd collected various other necessities such as aspirin and mentholyptic muscle rub for the occasional aches and pains during the night. He wasn't going to use Elise's personal care items and there was no reason to buy a second set of everything when he had a perfectly good set of his own.

And for that matter, he replaced the travel-size shampoo and shaving-cream containers with the full-size ones in his shower. No point in purchasing more of them, either.

His miniature DVD player landed on the bed—never knew when he'd feel a hankering for a shoot 'em up action movie. He tossed a couple of his favorites on top of the stack. Grabbed a lint brush to deal with her cats' hair. And headed out to the garage for a bigger bag. Or two.

ELISE WENT ABOUT the rest of her day the same as usual. By the time she was showered—having taken extra minutes to remove the decorative towels on the second rack in the big bathroom and replace them with a usable set for Joe, scrub the toilet and the tub, throw the rug in the wash, scour the sink and put all her essentials away in drawers and cabinets—both the crib sheets and the changing table had arrived as promised and were waiting in brown-paper-wrapped packages on the small porch connected to her side door.

Because it would take less time, she made the beds first—interrupted by a couple of trips to the kitchen to see what she had enough of to make for two for dinner.

Not much of anything.

Maybe Joe wouldn't be home to eat. He'd only said they'd take meals together when they were both here.

Perhaps she should go out. There'd been a movie or two she'd been meaning to see. She was wearing her new denim maternity jeans and white eyelet peasant top for the first time. She should show them off.

As she made up the cribs, Samantha, taking advantage of one lowered crib rail, jumped up into the middle of the partially placed sheet.

"Oh, no, girl, these aren't for you," Elise chided, hugging the cat to her chest as she gave the reprimand. Adding some behind-the-ear scratches and a kiss or two, she hoped Samantha had gotten the message.

And furthermore, she added to herself hours later as she put the changing table together, Joe wasn't coming "home" to eat, sleep or do anything else. This wasn't his home. It was hers. It was only—

"Can I help?"

Elise dropped the screwdriver on her bare toes. And bit back a yelp. "How'd you get in?"

Darin left the room. Oh, dear. Her cats hated him. This was never going to work.

"I used my key."

Turning, she saw the single key on the small coin chain she'd given him when she'd bought the house. She'd felt safer knowing that someone she trusted had a way in.

"Oh." Elise picked up the screwdriver, engaged it and twisted it with a vengeance. "Good," she said.

"Can I help with that?" he repeated.

She finished tightening the bolt and picked up another. "No, I've got it," she told him. "I moved my things out of the drawers in the front bedroom. And the blue towels in the bathroom are yours. I cleared room on the shelf in the shower, and the top right drawer is empty for you."

Another bolt tight. Three more to go, right the unit, slide in the drawers and she was done.

"Should you be doing that?"

It sounded as though he was still right behind.

"It came in parts," she told him. And she'd moved them from the box on the side porch to the back room one by one. "Nothing too heavy."

Elise waited through two long minutes of silence before she turned around.

He was gone.

AFTER A THOROUGH SEARCH of the pantry, refrigerator and freezer, Joe made a trip to the grocery store. He might have asked if he could pick something up for her, but wasn't sure bothering her was a good idea at the moment. He had the experience of fifteen years of lunches, occasional dinners and office chat to go on. He knew what Elise liked and disliked. He hoped. As much to the point, he had to have at least one frozen pizza waiting for a middle-of-the-night emergency—not that he'd ever once risen in the middle of the night to make one— and a bag of freshly ground breakfast-blend coffee for the morning. The rest he could wing and if he bought a lot, she wouldn't have to shop by herself and lug in the bags.

Making the best of a good day gone awry, he added a pound of ground beef to the pile. Elise had a built-in grill to the left of her garage. He'd grill dinner tonight. Throwing in a couple of cans of baked beans, he made a point to circle back and collect a couple of bags of freshly cut vegetables and some ranch dip. Elise had a soft spot for carrot and celery sticks.

The last thing he added to his cart, after the box of cat treats, was a twelve-pack of beer.

Joe pulled into the drive just after four, careful to park on the side opposite of where her car would be parked in the garage. Whistling, enjoying the light breeze coming off the river across the street, he figured he could do this for a few months. Especially if it meant that life as they knew it at B&R would be secure and back to normal at the end of that time.

He'd made many sacrifices for and investments in the company over the years. This one was really quite small. Considering.

A beer. A freshly grilled burger. Elise in his sight so he didn't have to worry about her doing something foolish and harming herself. The evening was shaping up.

The first thing he saw when he entered the kitchen, loaded down with plastic bags of perishables and other items, was the note on the kitchen table. It read: *Gone to GR. Meal is in the freezer. Help yourself.*

ELISE DIDN'T SEE JOE AGAIN that night. Wandering through a craft store on Twenty-eighth Street in Grand Rapids, she thought about the book she'd been reading the night before. The one now on the nightstand in the smallest bedroom in her house.

She thought about the wallpaper border waiting to be put up in the babies' room. Already starting to bulge at a little over three months, she might not have much longer to climb a ladder.

She longed for the comfort of her family room, a quiet dinner of veggies and bread with peanut butter, and a tall glass of decaffeinated iced tea. Instead, she was wasting time in the city until she could show up at a restaurant by herself, the choice about which she cared not a whit, and do something she detested—eating out alone.

Because her best friend from college had decided to be her roommate. After all this time.

Her new roommate was in his room, door closed, when she arrived home at a little after eight. The light was on. She could hear voices, but saw no sign of a meal or refreshments having been prepared in the kitchen, though there was an overabundance of groceries.

And the bathroom smelled like his aftershave.

Back out to the kitchen to get a bottle of water

to take to bed with her, she had to go by his room a second time to get to hers—and still heard talking.

Had he brought a television set?

His laptop?

For all she knew, he had a woman in there.

JOE OPENED HIS DOOR a crack when he turned off the light that first night. He was here to help if she got in trouble, so he had to be able to hear if his services were needed.

And he stood in the dining room, just beyond the entry to the hall that led back to the bathroom when, at 3:00 a.m., she was up being sick. And again at 5:00 a.m.

Why anyone would want to do this to herself was beyond him. Not so much the morning sickness—he knew she couldn't have predicted the degree to which that would hit her—but the whole kid thing. The noise, the chaos. The lack of control.

The entire concept gave him an urge to run.

"YOU'RE UP EARLY."

Half-asleep, Joe plugged in the automatic coffeemaker he'd filled the night before. He turned to see Elise sitting at the table drinking a glass of orange juice and reading the Sunday paper. Samantha was curled up in her lap.

"I shoot hoops with Kenny at eight."

"Just today, or every Sunday?"

If he hadn't heard the violence of her retching he never would have believed this woman hadn't just come from a peaceful night's sleep. Already showered, dressed in a looser sundress than he was used to seeing on her, hair all fluffed and picked the way it was every day, makeup as understated as always on her perfect features, she could have been a model on her way to a photo shoot.

"Every Sunday. We rent a court at the Y."

Joe wasn't sure what to do with himself while the coffee perked—certainly not his usual practice of sitting in a chair and nodding off for a couple of last minutes. Neither could he join her and ask for the sports section. With his muscle shirt, nylon shorts, bare feet and mussed hair, he felt at a decided disadvantage. He hadn't even brushed his teeth yet.

"I thought you'd still be asleep," he said.

She peered at him over the top of the paper. "I have wallpapering to do today. Besides, you know I'm an early riser."

Normally, yeah, but if he'd been up sick…

Before he could formulate any kind of reply, Elise's head was buried back behind the paper.

And that wasn't like her at all.

ELISE MISSED HER STEP on the ladder when she heard Joe's car in the drive. It was just before she was ready to break for lunch. The three-foot-long piece of pasted border in her hand—specially cut for over the doorway—got tangled as she grasped the metal side of the ladder, her heart in her throat.

She'd been so careful not to fall.

And now almost had—thanks to him.

"Tell me you're not climbing up on that thing."

He'd made it into the house in record time. And could obviously see the new paper garnishing the upper rim of the room's walls.

"I still have perfect balance."

"But stand to lose a whole lot more than dignity if you fall."

Still fresh from her scare, knowing that this time he was right, Elise felt heat creep into her skin. She averted her eyes and said nothing.

"In the future, I'd be happy to help with any items that put you or the babies in danger."

She still couldn't look at him. "Thank you."

"I mean it, Elise."

God, she hated this. Hated her lack of control. When she'd had things so carefully planned.

"Then could you please hang this last section for me before the paste dries and clots?"

The seam wasn't quite straight when he stepped off the ladder several moments later.

Elise didn't say a word.

"HOW ABOUT SOME LUNCH?" Joe asked, carrying out the last of the morning's project's supplies.

When Elise only jerked her head in a nod, he

stopped, paste container, squeegee and razor blade knife in hand and waited for her to look at him.

"I wasn't asking you to prepare it for me," he added. "I'd be happy to take you out to the Levee, or anywhere else you'd like to go. Or to whip up some tuna-salad sandwiches."

"We've never gone out to eat on a Sunday before, and we certainly aren't starting now. The deal was we'd eat together if we were both here, because it's more economically feasible."

He didn't remember being that succinct about it, but okay.

"Well, we're both here," he said.

She looked surprised for a second, then, "You put those things away, I'll make up the tuna."

He didn't really like tuna all that much, but he wasn't about to say so.

"I'll meet you in the kitchen," he told her. And as she was about to walk away, added, "Oh, and Elise?"

"Yeah?"

"I miss my friend. Is there any way she'll be in the kitchen when I get there?"

The long look she gave him didn't bode well. But Joe was hopeful just the same.

His friend Elise wasn't there when he sat down at the round table in the corner set for two, but halfway through the chips and sandwiches as they talked about the new pay tech possibilities, Joe could sense Elise starting to relax.

"Have you told your family you're staying here?" she asked him, changing the subject. "I only ask because the phone rang while you were gone and it dawned on me that I don't know if you've given out the number or what you'll want me to tell people."

Complications bred everywhere. He could count on it.

"No," he said, and then, off the top of his head, "I don't see any reason to tell anyone about our arrangement. Everyone calls me on my cell, anyway. Why risk speculation where there is none?"

"I tell my parents everything—" She broke off, alarm on her face.

"I have no problem with that," Joe said quickly. "I imagine they're good listeners."

"You think I'm strange. Morbid or something."

"I think you're an amazingly strong and determined woman who believes enough in an afterlife to receive comfort from it."

The response awarded him his first smile of the day. "Thank you."

He felt better, too. A lot.

AT SIX, JOE OFFERED to grill the burgers he'd bought the day before. Elise suggested that they eat on the enclosed porch off the kitchen and busied herself in the kitchen with the rest of the meal. He might have felt claustrophobic with the domesticity of it all if the woman he was coupled with weren't his business partner.

They were working together for the good of B&R. Just as they always had.

"So once you'd gone through all the preliminary stuff and determined that this was what you wanted to do, did the actual process follow immediately?" Joe asked, slowly sipping his second beer while Elise finished eating. He never would've asked, but she'd brought up the subject, delineating the steps she'd taken almost as though it were crucial that he understand how carefully she'd planned.

She needn't have worried. This was Elise. Of course she'd planned. Hell, the woman would predetermine her dreams at night if such a thing were possible.

And the trait was one of the things that he relied upon most heavily. Without her careful planning, B&R would never have been born, let alone grown into a company that could very well become public in the years to come.

"It could have happened almost immediately," she said slowly, "but I wasn't too fond of the sperm bank idea—it seemed kind of like a crapshoot to me. I wanted a little more control over the DNA and heredity choice for my child."

If he'd been chewing he probably would've choked.

"I assumed when you said you didn't know the father, that…"

"I don't know whose sperm was actually used." She finished off the last of her beans, put down her fork. "But I know that it came from one of the five men I interviewed and chose to help me with this. Each one had agreed, for a higher sum of course, to contribute sperm. Only the clinic knows which of the five they used."

"You've met the father, then?" Joe suddenly wasn't nearly as relaxed as he'd been. Must be just getting stiff from the morning workout with Kenny.

"Not in person," she said, sitting back. "The clinic ran an ad, which I paid for, then referred the applicants to me. They all agreed to background checks—and to chatting with me on the phone. We also e-mailed a bit. I didn't want the communication to get too personal, just enough to feel I was making an educated choice."

He supposed, once he thought about it, he wouldn't have expected anything different from her. Control from a distance—that about summed her up.

Or he'd thought it had.

After everything he'd learned about Elise in the past month, he was no longer as sure. Beneath that calm, controlled exterior lived a woman who could throw up and pretend she hadn't, hang wallpaper, and then visit her parents' graves to tell them she had a new roommate.

"I'm assuming they're all either in college or are college graduates?" Not that it mattered. He had no stake in this. No real interest, other than seeing his partner through it safely.

"No. But they all have goals and good work ethics. Most importantly, their family history is sound."

"Any of them married?"

"I didn't ask, but one of them said he was. He'd answered the ad so he could earn the money to take his wife on a belated honeymoon to Hawaii. Six years ago, it seems, they eloped and went back to work the day afterward."

"Did any of them have kids?"

"Again, not a question I asked. These were potential donors of something I needed, nothing more," she told him, her voice clear.

No fatherhood involved, Joe translated, and wondered if he should feel sorry for the guys, for her, for the children—or not.

CHAPTER SIX

"YOUR DOCTOR CALLED just after you left. She wants you to call her back as soon as possible."

Elise, going over a multitiered proposal for the bankers Joe was courting, glanced up as he presented himself at her office door Monday morning.

Keeping the fear he'd just elicited firmly under wraps, she said, "Fine," and pretended to see the pages in front of her. "I believe the vendor expansion is a solid idea and is going to really benefit us, but we probably need to consider developing our own in-house HR department."

"Elise…"

"I've been going over this Michigan Local Bank proposal. I'm not sure we want to outsource services such as recruitment and procedure and policy manual creation. Those things are too personal, too specialized, not to have day-to-day control over them."

Joe, every bit the successful and confident businessman in his pressed dark slacks, silk tie and expensive shoes, crossed to her desk. He stood over her, hands on his hips. "Call your doctor."

"I will." She was glad he couldn't see the sweat trickling down the back of her sleeveless cotton blouse—or what felt like a puddle of it forming at the elastic waistband of the colorful flowing skirt she'd put on because it was one of the few that still fit. "When you calculate the number of employee hours it's going to cost us to provide recruiting services, particularly in the beginning with the start-up learning curve—"

A large male hand came down on top of the report. "Now."

Elise remembered that he was giving up his personal life for several months to help her out of the mess she'd made of hers, and bit her lip.

"Five minutes isn't going to make a difference," she said instead, "no matter what she has to tell me." She refused to think about the tests the doctor had run on Friday, the various results they'd been hoping *not* to find. She looked straight at him. "I need normalcy somewhere in my life, Joe, and at the moment, here is about the only place I'm likely to even have a chance of finding it." Her home was certainly not the safe haven it once had been. "Right now, I'd like to discuss business with my partner. You've got another meeting with Michigan Local this week and I want to make certain we're equipped to support your promises one hundred percent if they sign."

He frowned, stared her down and sat. "Fair enough. What are you thinking?"

"Tamara has extensive experience with policy

and procedure manuals from her work with the National Organization for Association Management. She's done all our background checks whenever we've hired anyone. I've had her handle the last couple of potential-employee interviews. She's reliable, conscientious, works well under pressure and makes sound decisions. I'd like to promote her to head up an HR department, which, at the moment, would consist only of her with the promise to hire at least one assistant for her by the end of the year if this pans out."

The end of the year. Would she be healthy then? And, more importantly, the mother of four healthy babies?

"Can we afford to pay her what the position would require?"

Elise peered at the figures she'd run up—more than once. "You've bid Michigan Local at a four percent admin fee."

"It's lower than most of our accounts, but the payroll's also bigger, so it'd bring in more revenue overall."

"And still within industry standard," she added. She hadn't been complaining. "It's fair, but just not going to support this department on its own. Nor should it. In order to make this work, we'll need more companies using it, supporting it. And that's going to take some build time."

"You wouldn't have suggested this if you didn't have a plan. What've you got in mind?"

He knew her well. Today, Elise took comfort in that.

"If we cut our personal monthly sales bonus by a quarter percent, we'll stay out of the red."

"You can't afford a pay cut right now."

She held up the report she'd tackled first thing that morning. "This is the best work you've ever done, Joe. We can't afford not to give it every chance to succeed. We've worked a long time to get to this point. We've got the personnel, the longevity to make it happen. We're ready."

"You can't afford to take a pay cut."

She glanced down, swallowed. Started to feel the effects of the immediate worry her doctor's phone call caused in the form of renewed morning sickness. She finally managed to say, "With you living at my house, I can." Meeting his gaze head-on, completely serious, she said, "You have to give me your word that you'll be there till the first of the year."

If all went as planned, their salaries would increase considerably on that date.

"You're paying half the utilities, splitting groceries, and if I don't have to hire any in-home care at all this year, I should be fine."

"You already have my word." Joe leaned forward, both arms resting on the front edge of her desk, his gaze completely clear. "I already made that decision on Saturday. If anything happens to you, we could lose B&R. Case closed."

Elise was afraid she was going to cry. If nausea

didn't get her, her oversensitized hormones would. "I can't stand being a burden."

"Hey." Joe waited until she looked up at him—which she did eventually, reluctantly. "You are a friend, a valuable and valued partner. You gave me the means to make a dream into reality, covered for me when I showed up one too many times hung over after my divorce. You've worked long hours unceasingly for ten years, planning, developing, overseeing. You invested in this partnership, Elise, and now it's time to collect a well-earned dividend."

She loved that he spoke in financial terms. They were as familiar to her as food and water—as safe and controlled as anything in life could ever be.

"I'll talk to Tamara this afternoon," was all she said.

"Good." Joe stood. "Now call your doctor."

"I will."

He remained in place.

"Right now."

He wasn't leaving.

"Just as soon as you go."

"Considering the fact that I have a sizable investment here, and a responsibility to oversee the outcome, I deem it necessary that I stay."

The man was going to drive her certifiably insane. Long before she had four crying babies to take their shot.

He was also cramping her style, taking away the

one thing she'd always had—from the time she'd woken up screaming in pain in an Arkansas hospital with no memory of the fire that had just taken the lives of everyone she loved—her independence.

As she picked up the phone and pushed the speed dial button, Elise told herself to get used to it. She needed him.

"Dr. Braden, please." Joe looked pointedly at the shaking pencil in her hand and Elise dropped it. If the news was bad...

Joe was here.

THE OBSTETRICIAN HAD a couple of things to discuss with Elise. "But first," she said, prolonging Elise's stress, "the good news. Your liver and kidneys are fine. There's no sign yet of gestational hypertension. Of course it's early yet—the chances of the disease occurring rise considerably the further the pregnancy progresses. Like I told you, fifty percent of quad pregnancies result in some degree of high blood pressure, toxemia or pre-eclampsia, so this is something we'll be watching closely."

Elise was used to doctors, had spent more time, more holidays, with them than with friends during her teen years. This one scared her.

And engendered her complete faith.

Dr. Braden had told her on her first visit that gestational hypertension was the number-one cause

of premature deliveries with a multiple pregnancies. She was glad the doctor was taking the
threat seriously.

"And on that note, I need you to come back in
for another diabetes test," Dr. Braden continued,
her voice completely lacking in emotion. Good or
bad.

Elise wanted to ask if there was a problem, but
was too conscious of Joe standing there to do so.

"Friday's test came back positive, but it's not a
sure indicator."

Diabetes. She couldn't even remember all the
complications that could arise from that. Not even
fourteen weeks along and it was starting already.

"Okay."

Why had she ever thought she could do this?

Ignoring Joe's intense stare, she picked up her
pencil again, pretending everything was just fine.

"And I want to see another ultrasound," Dr.
Braden said as though reading off a list. "I've
scheduled you here in the office for ten o'clock
next Friday. Can you make that?"

"Yes."

"Terrific. Everything sounded fine on Friday, I
think we're good to go, but I want to keep a close
watch on the growth and placement of the babies.
You can expect at least monthly ultrasounds."

Oh. Well, fine. It could be worse.

Much worse.

"So?" Joe could barely contain his frustration by the time Elise hung up the phone.

"What?" She looked up at him as though she had no idea what he wanted.

"'Okay' and 'yes' were the sum total of your half of that conversation."

"Oh. Well, everything's fine."

"She asked you to call her ASAP to tell you that your condition is status quo?"

The woman was maddening. Independent to the point of insult. They were going to have a talk about being considerate. And cooperative. He had a job to do and he was damn well going to do it properly.

"I have to have another diabetes test—I'll do that tomorrow—and then a week from Friday I'm scheduled for an ultrasound."

"What's that for?"

"To monitor the babies' measurements, mostly."

"Does it hurt?"

Her smile relaxed him a bit. "Not at all. I've already had one. They run a camera kind of thing over my belly and the sound waves vibrate back a picture."

Important. And not too invasive.

"Okay, what time?"

"Ten. Why?"

"I'm coming."

"You most certainly are not."

Joe almost stormed around the desk to make his point clear, but thought better of it just in time.

Instead, he settled on a corner of her desk and turned to look at her.

"It's going to be just you and me through much of this, Elise," he told her, lowering his voice to the level he used when trying to convince his mother to follow the diet her kidney doctor gave her. "I'm accepting a bit of responsibility. It's only fair that I be as educated as possible about what's going on. How will I know what to watch for? What to expect? If I'm informed, I'll know whether to be alarmed or just thrust smelling salts under your nose if you pass out."

"I'm not going to pass out. Have a seizure, maybe, but no passing out."

He got to his feet, alarmed all over again. "A seizure?"

"I'm joking, Joe."

Then why wasn't there any sign of humor about her, a curve in those tense lips, light in those concerned eyes.

He started a mental list of things to ask her doctor at the next appointment. "Seizures" was at the top.

"Well, I'm not," he told her now. "I'll leave the room for anything too private, but I'd feel a lot better if you'd agree to allow me to attend your appointments with you."

"Is this a contingency to the deal?"

He wanted to say yes. Almost gave in to the temptation. "No."

"But it would make this whole thing easier on you?"

"Yes."

She considered him for a long moment. "How about if you go with me next Friday and then we'll see after that?"

It was more than he'd expected. Joe grinned. Agreed. And left to reschedule the meeting he had on the following Friday with a chain of learning centers.

Now that his mission was accomplished and he was actually sitting at his desk contemplating what he'd be doing a week from Friday, Joe broke out into a cold sweat.

He couldn't lose Elise. B&R was his life. He'd sacrifice just about anything to keep the business healthy. Even if the toll it took was great.

He could curse his partner for getting herself into this mess. And yet, he couldn't really. She'd signed on for one baby, not four.

And after hearing the miraculous and tragic story of her youth, he couldn't find fault with any of the decisions she'd made.

Joe jumped up, grabbed his keys, as another thought occurred to him. He didn't just want Elise healthy and her pregnancy successful for B&R, he wanted it for Elise.

And as he drove to his first appointment, two facts continued to hound him. These babies were important to Elise.

That made them important to him. B&R aside.

Like it or not, he was in this with her.

January first couldn't come fast enough.

ON WEDNESDAY NIGHT a week later, Elise made chicken picatta for dinner. The dish was one of her favorites—and something she only made when she had someone to cook for, which, since Joe and Kelly's divorce, was rarely. She tossed a salad, adding a little cabbage for extra zing, and took the time to prepare risotto from scratch.

They'd fallen into a routine, she and Joe. She wasn't all that unhappy with it. Almost as if they were at work, they allowed room for each other's idiosyncrasies without judgment or ridicule. She was quiet when she got up at five and was gone before he needed to get to the coffeepot at six-thirty. He kept the noise down after eleven at night. She made room for his frozen pizzas and he put up with Darin and Samantha. She cooked dinner—just as she did on Fridays for their staff. And he cleaned up afterward—as he used to do at work before the women insisted on doing it for him.

Joe had always had that effect on women, except for Elise. As a rule they vied for opportunities to fawn all over him. To spoil him. Take care of him. Elise taught him how to take care of himself. And expected him to do so.

Every night, after she left the office between 5:30 and 6:00, she came straight home to make dinner, for which he showed up at seven, completely famished. They never spoke of the meal—never had "see you at dinner" or "what's for dinner?" conversations. She always cooked and he always arrived in time to eat.

But not tonight. Seven came and went. Elise turned down the heat on the rice and, dousing the chicken with a little extra sauce, covered it and set the oven to warm. She fed the cats. At seven-thirty, because her babies were getting fussy, she ate some of the salad. And by eight, added a dish of past-its-prime, sticky risotto to the offering. At nine, she cut the chicken up into little pieces, bagging them in separate portions for future meals for Darin and Samantha.

When the clock hit ten, she took Samantha and Darin and went in to bed. She wasn't angry. Why should she be? Joe owed her nothing. They weren't a family. Had no reason to share meals or to count on sharing meals.

They just ate together when they both happened to be in the place at mealtime. Strictly for economic purposes.

She heard him pull in at ten-thirty. He knew she went to bed at eleven. Elise jumped up, pulled on sweats and a t-shirt over her nightgown. She'd forgotten to water the plants. Every Sunday, Wednesday and Friday, immediately after dinner, she watered all the plants in her house.

He came through the kitchen just as she was getting at the philodendron over the sink.

"Smells good in here."

That rankled. "Chicken picatta." *Where the hell were you?* She stopped the thought, revised it. *Where were you?* And didn't voice it, either. It was none of her business where he was.

And that was as it should be. As it must be if they were going to survive all these months under the same roof.

"I'm sorry I missed it."

She spun around. He was through the kitchen, at the arch leading into the dining room that would take him to his bedroom. He had his tie in his hand.

"Me, too." Only because he would've liked it.

He turned back. "You sound as if you're on edge. What's up?"

"I'm not on edge." She couldn't have sounded more innocent if she'd been a newborn babe. She *was* innocent. At least if motivation and desire had any say in it.

"Yes, you do. 'Fess up. I left my dirty socks somewhere and it made you mad, right?"

His hair was mussed. And the top two buttons of his shirt were undone.

"I don't sound on edge," she repeated.

He studied her for a time and shrugged. "Have it your way." He started toward his room, then faced her again. "But don't hold it against me if I keep doing whatever it is I did—"

"Dinner was ruined waiting for you."

Elise could have bitten her tongue for letting the

words escape. She came across like a poor rendition
of a bitchy housewife—not like a business partner
who appreciated his assistance in a personal matter.

He took a couple of steps toward her. "I should
have called."

Elise faced the faucet, refilled her watering can.
"No, you shouldn't. We aren't like that."

"Like what?" His voice was only a few feet
behind her.

"Like people who owe each other explanations."

"For the time being we live in the same resi-
dence." Joe's voice, as calm as she wished hers
was, irritated the crap out of her. "It's common
decency to let the other person know if we're going
to be out. I'm sorry. It won't happen again."

She slowly faced him, ashamed and grateful at
the same time. "I'm overreacting."

"You had no reason to think I wasn't expecting
dinner tonight, no reason not to prepare one."

He was right. Which meant she was, too. Elise
almost giggled with relief. She wasn't getting
too proprietary or acting out of place. She'd
merely been frustrated by the inconvenience. As
anybody would be.

"Did you have a good time?" she asked him,
much more charitable now that she didn't have to
worry about her reactions.

"Relatively. Melanie's an intelligent woman,
fun. I was just a little preoccupied tonight. Thanks
for asking."

With that, he wished her good-night and went to his room.

While she'd been home waiting dinner for him, he'd been with a woman.

The anger she'd thought truly quelled burst into flames once more.

Anger at his inconsiderate actions. But more, anger at herself for caring. She'd better control that before she wrecked everything—for him, for her, and for the babies who were counting on her to bring them safely into the world.

Still, her last thought, as she drifted off to sleep cradling her slightly protruding stomach, was to wonder if Joe had made love with Melanie, the paragon, that night.

CHAPTER SEVEN

ON FRIDAY JOE WENT TO WORK as usual and presented himself at Elise's office at the exact time she'd specified in the note she'd left on the kitchen table that morning. The note had also said that her doctor had called and she didn't have diabetes.

He hadn't seen her, except in passing at the office, since Wednesday. She'd gone shopping for maternity clothes the night before and he'd played racquetball with a client-turned-friend. He'd stayed afterward to have a drink and talk shop.

And now, waiting outside the room while Elise prepared for the test, he considered exchanging his current plans for another visit to a local bar. They'd driven separately, at Elise's insistence. He could head right out that door.

A very pregnant woman walked by—if you could call the painful-looking waddle walking— with a little kid on either side of her, small hands clasped in hers. She was going to have at least two in diapers at the same time—possibly three. Big boxes of different-size disposables, being at the beck and call of rashes and smells that needed attention, lugging all the stuff everywhere, fussing when things weren't attended to quickly enough.

Joe shuddered, held the door to the waiting room open for her.

Elise was going to have four in diapers at once.

He loosened his tie, unbuttoned the top of his shirt.

He, of all people, didn't belong here. Kelly would laugh uproariously if she could see him.

He tried not to think of Elise on the other side of the door, getting undressed, of him seeing her that way. He really hadn't thought this through in enough detail. Seeing Elise in a state of undress would be embarrassing. For her and for him.

In sweats, fine. Without a shower, great. But not nude.

Not that she would be. Patients were always covered with at least a sheet in hospitals. But if he knew she was nude underneath them?

Sweat beaded on his forehead.

What the hell was the matter with him?

They hadn't said ten words to each other in two days. This was a business transaction. He needed to get a grip.

"Mr. Bennett? We're ready for you now." The technician, dressed in green scrubs, looked to be in her early thirties. She seemed kind. Joe liked her immediately—couldn't run out on her.

Hands in his pockets, he pasted on his best salesman smile and entered the dimly lit room.

Television monitors were set up in what he supposed were strategic places. He had a clear view of two of them and kept his gaze firmly focused there, doing his best to ignore his peripheral vision and a view of his business partner that made him entirely too uncomfortable.

Still wearing the loose white blouse and elastic waistband black skirt she'd had on the last time he'd seen her, she was lying on the table, her belly exposed. Her skin was white, silky-looking, beautiful. Unscarred. He had an urge to kiss her there.

And then the show started. Flashes of shadows appeared on the screen, indiscernible black and white and gray shapes. And a ruler.

"Okay." The technician's voice penetrated the eerily quiet room. An arrow appeared over one of the larger gray shadows. "Here's Baby A." The ruler moved. She called out head circumference, arm and leg measurements—all the while pointing at things that barely resembled a swimming blob, let alone a human being, albeit in the beginning stages.

"And," the woman said, her voice rising a notch, "we've got a boy!"

"A boy?" Elise's emotion-filled cry was foreign to him. She seemed to lean forward, but with only his peripheral view, he couldn't be certain. "Are you sure?"

"Yep," the woman said, zooming in. "There's your proof."

A boy? Joe leaned in closer. A boy? Where? He stared at the monitor. Didn't really matter if he could make out babies or not. This trained professional could. Elise was having a son. The concept was almost impossible to grasp.

"On to Baby B," the woman was saying when Joe tuned in again. His mouth was dry. He wondered if there was any water nearby. He let his gaze wander away from the measurements and…proof that his partner was really planning to give birth to four new people.

Were her kidneys there, too? And her liver? He wouldn't mind looking at them.

"Another boy!" The technician sounded as if she was solely responsible for the news.

"Two boys!" Elise giggled.

And Joe looked straight at her. Her gaze was focused on the one screen she could see. And then her gaze sought his—just as he'd realized he was smiling at her.

"I'm having two sons, Joe," she said, no hint of embarrassment in her tone, no hint of anything but pure joy.

For the first time since the ordeal began, Joe was glad he was there.

"TWO GIRLS AND TWO BOYS, can you believe it?" Elise was still flying high when he walked with her out to their cars half an hour later, the films they'd given her clasped tightly in her hands.

Squinting in the early-August sun, she glanced over at him, and he reached to put an arm around her, then caught himself just in time. He scratched his head, instead.

He couldn't believe any of this. Kept waiting to awake from the nightmare, get up, drive in to work and find Elise as slim as ever at her desk. No fire, no tragedy, no chaotic home life in sight.

"What are you going to name them?" he said now.

"I just found out what I'm having twenty minutes ago, Joe," she said, chuckling. "And I've been a little preoccupied since."

"And I know you." He worked up a grin. "You've had plans for any eventuality already in place."

They'd reached her car. Only then did Joe notice that she'd sobered.

"You're right, of course." She paused, as though considering her answer. Then, "I'm naming three of them after my brother and sisters. The fourth is going to be called Thomas."

The babies—her new family—were to be named after the family she'd lost. So easy for him to forget, to see her as the calm, efficient woman she'd always been, while every moment of every day Elise carried burdens he'd never even imagined.

"What were your brother and sisters' names?"

"Danny, Ellen and Grace."

He liked all three. "And Thomas? Who's he? Your father?"

She smiled again, a faraway look on her face. "Thomas—Dr. Fuller. He's the doctor who made me what I am today. The one who provided so much more than medical care."

"I'd like to meet him someday."

Elise blinked. Looked startled, as though the idea had never crossed her mind.

And why should it have? Until this moment it had never occurred to him, either.

"That'd be a little difficult," she said, unlocking her car. "He and his wife, Elizabeth, live in Arkansas."

Of course. That was where she'd said her family home had been.

"Do you ever see them?"

"Not since I moved here. They keep saying they're going to come out for a visit. And I've thought about going back there, but I can never quite make myself do it."

He could understand that. Although they were people she loved, being back in the place where her entire family had perished might be too upsetting. And too strong a reminder of what she herself had been through.

"So you talk to them often?" he asked.

"At least once a month, lately, more."

"They know about the babies?"

"They knew about the plan the second I realized I was seriously thinking about going through with it."

They really *were* close. Heat emanated from the

blacktop, adding to the ninety-degree temperatures. It couldn't be good for her to be standing out here. And he had to get back to work—Sam Watterson was waiting to go over a bid with him.

Yet Joe didn't want to leave her. There was so much more he wanted to know about this woman.

"What was their reaction?" he asked just as she was about to climb into her car.

"It's hard to tell," she told him, frowning. "They're always so upbeat with me, you know, like playing cheerleader is their role in my life."

"Is that bad? Everyone needs a cheerleader."

Elise ran fingers through her short, windblown hair. "No, it's not bad," she said. "It's just that I'd prefer honesty sometimes, you know? If it's bad, tell me it's bad so I can start dealing with it."

"You don't think Thomas would tell you if he thought you were going to do something that could harm you?"

He recognized the look that came to her eyes then. She usually got it when he scored a point. Of course, it was usually over some business plan they'd been concocting.

"Of course he would."

"So what did he say about your carrying quadruplets?"

"Besides the fact that my stomach is going to stretch beyond what I'd ever believe it could?"

Joe hadn't needed to hear that. The image was a little too intimate for him to handle. "Yeah," he said, trying not to think about his earlier and completely embarrassing urge to kiss her.

"He told me to follow my doctor's orders, to take all my vitamins, and said that I can't question the Lord's timing. I wanted a big family and I'm getting one. Who am I to look a gift horse in the mouth?"

"He said that?"

"Not just like that, but basically."

Joe wasn't sure if he liked this guy. Not that it was any of his business, but maybe hers was a case when the gift horse *should* be looked at. Carefully.

Something else she'd said occurred to him, distracting him from thoughts and feelings that were far too complicated.

"Why aren't you taking the vitamins?

"I am. Haven't missed one."

"I've never seen them."

"They're in my nightstand drawer."

Looking at him in puzzlement, she shook her head and said, "I have to get back." She climbed in behind the wheel. "I'm meeting with Tamara again at one."

"Yeah." Joe held the top of her door, meaning to close it. He had that meeting with Sam. "You want to have lunch first?" he heard himself say, though he had no idea why. It couldn't be a good practice to get into, this resisting a return from personal to business.

And no matter how it might look, there *was* no personal. Between him and Elise everything was business. Wasn't it?

"No, thanks, Joe," she said, smiling her refusal. "I made oriental chicken salad for the staff when I got in this morning. I told Tamara to be sure and save me some."

And just like that, she'd become Elise Richardson, of Bennett and Richardson Professional Employee Organization—his business partner.

As he followed her Corvette back to the office, Joe was relieved things had returned to normal.

AWAKE AT TWO O'CLOCK the next morning, Elise lay in bed and prayed that the pizza she'd suggested she and Joe have for dinner so they could watch a movie while they ate—and avoid any awkward personal conversation—wasn't suddenly going to come out the way it had gone in.

She didn't feel sick. But nothing else kept her awake these days. She was exhausted by bedtime and asleep almost before she shut her eyes.

The only bodily urge she felt was the need to pee. She'd never had to get up in the night to do that. Not even as a kid.

Kids. She had four of them. Two boys and two girls. Real and living and growing inside her.

Elise turned over.

She'd gained ten of the fifty pounds Dr. Braden was hoping for. They must all be resting on her bladder.

Memories of her sister, Baby Grace, flashed through her mind. How warm she'd been the times

Mama had let her hold her. The golden blond hair and big brown eyes, just like Mama's. The rest of them had dark hair and lighter eyes like Daddy.

She flipped around again, unable to find a comfortable position for her bladder. Samantha jumped down from the bed and joined Darin underneath it. Elise was going to have to get up and go to the bathroom.

And she hated that Joe might hear her moving around and think she was getting sick again. How embarrassing to have him standing around listening to her pee. Or asking her if she was sick, to which she'd have to tell him what she was doing.

Elise sat up, threw off the sheet—the only covering she could stand on the hot August night in a house too old for central air conditioning. This was ridiculous. She was a grown woman in her own home. If she had to go, she had to go.

CAREFUL TO TURN OFF the bathroom light before she opened the door when she was finished, Elise peered out into the darkened hallway. She'd really like a glass of milk. Did she dare risk the trip to the kitchen?

No lights were on. She didn't see any movement in the dining room. If Joe had gotten up, as he'd mentioned he'd done before when she'd been sick, he'd obviously gone back to bed.

Coast clear, Elise felt like a kid sneaking down to see Santa Claus on Christmas Eve. She tiptoed down the short, carpeted hall in her thigh-length sleeveless cotton nightgown. Two weeks ago, she'd have made the same walk in camisole and panties.

She didn't even dare *sleep* in such immodest comfort these days.

Rounding the corner, she took one last look toward his room. The door was open. But there was no sound coming from within—no rustling of covers, no movement.

Elise breathed easier, now thinking almost exclusively of that glass of milk, and almost tripped over a dining-room chair that was pulled out from its usual place up to the table. Almost fell on the man sitting in the chair, slumped over the table, sound asleep.

Or at least he was until Elise yelped. Awake instantly, Joe's arms were around Elise before she'd even realized what was happening, before she could step back.

"What's wrong?" he asked, getting to his feet.

"Uh, nothing," Elise mumbled against his chest. Her heart was pounding from the scare, her body doing all kinds of strange things as it lay pressed against his solid warmth.

As soon as she'd steadied herself, she pushed away from him.

But not before she'd felt evidence of his own obviously inadvertent physical reaction against her thighs.

"I was just going for some milk," she stammered, hurrying toward the kitchen.

Please, God, let him be gone when I get back.

Joe followed her to the kitchen. "I'd like some, too."

She grabbed another glass, splashed some milk into it—and some on the counter, too. Which she promptly wiped up with the cloth hanging over the faucet, hoping he hadn't seen this evidence of her nervousness. She'd only turned on the small light over the sink. Things would be easy to miss.

"You sure you're okay?" he asked, taking the gallon jug from her to finish the job.

"Yes, fine. No sickness for once." She sipped her milk, leaning back against the far counter.

"Guess those kids of yours are more discerning than you are."

"What do you mean by that?"

He downed most of the contents of his glass in one gulp. "They understand the value of a good pizza."

"'Good' being the operative word." Elise grinned at him, starting to relax a bit. Maybe she'd imagined Joe's reaction. Maybe she'd made the whole thing up. Maybe what she'd felt was his hipbone. She hadn't been with a man in so long, she could be excused for the mistake.

Joe certainly didn't seem to be anything other than his old self.

"Freshly prepared to order Hawaiian pizza holds no resemblance to something you get frozen from a box," she continued when he just raised a brow at her. "And it was hot and for dinner. Not cold, leftover, breakfast fare."

Milk gone, he set his glass on the counter, leaned against the sink, facing her, his arms crossed.

"So what's got you needing milk in the middle of the night?"

Elise stopped just short of saying "nothing." His tone was warm, caring. The night was long and dark. And this was Joe. Just Joe. Not that man she'd created in her mind in the dining room.

He was her business partner. There to see that she got this project completed successfully so she could do her work at B&R.

They'd been together for ten years and he'd never shown the least bit of interest in her as a woman.

If that didn't make him safe, she didn't know what would.

"Visions of my baby sister keep flashing through my mind," she finally admitted, the words foreign-feeling as they escaped her.

"Tell me about her."

"I don't remember all that much. I know I was excited that she was a girl. Couldn't wait for her to get home so I could help take care of her."

"Did you?"

"Some. But mostly Mama gave the baby jobs to Ellen. She was four years older than me. The household chores fell to me."

"And that made you mad?"

"Not really. I understood. Besides, I liked making dessert and that was one of the chores. I liked to iron back then, too, though that particular joy didn't last long."

"I don't like it, either. It's a good thing the wrinkled look is in."

Elise chuckled. Then sobered, peering at him over the rim of her glass in the mostly moonlit room.

"That's why Grace and Ellen were in the same room the night of the fire," she said softly. "Two of us girls had to share, and Mama decided it should be Grace and Ellen since it was Ellen's job to watch over the baby."

His eyes darkened. "I'm sorry."

Elise put her empty glass on the counter. She meant to stop right there. She'd shared some of her memories—more than she ever had. It was enough. And yet… "I keep picturing what the fire must have done to her." Her voice breaking over the words, Elise hugged her arms around her middle. "That sweet baby face, and hair, and tiny body. Did she suffer much? Or did it get her so quickly she never completely woke up? Never knew what hit her?"

"Those are things you aren't ever going to know," Joe said. The caring in his voice seemed to wrap around her. Warming her. "The main thing is to know that she's not suffering now. And if she did suffer then, you can bet there were angels there, too, helping her along, comforting her, gathering her up and taking her home."

Tears filled her eyes as she stared at him. She couldn't believe he'd said that. Since when did Joe believe in angels?

She'd known him for fifteen years—spirituality had never once come up.

"Thank you," she whispered when she could. "I think that's the nicest thing anyone has ever said to me about that night."

Such a simple thing. Baby Grace had been tended by angels that night. You'd think she'd have thought of it herself.

But no, it was Joe, her business partner, who found a way to unlock her heart.

CHAPTER EIGHT

AT BREAKFAST THE NEXT morning, Joe did his best to think about business. With the new vendor list they were compiling—and an HR department to flesh out—they had a lot to talk about. So what if it was Saturday, his sacred day to play. Times weren't normal.

She'd invited him to join her for an omelet and fruit when he'd passed through the kitchen in shorts and a T-shirt on his way out to his car. It'd seemed churlish to refuse. His canoe could wait.

"Tamara was thrilled with the HR proposal," Elise said, eating slowly. "She had some great ideas and believes that, for now, she'll have no problem handling things herself."

She looked more beautiful than usual, he thought. Softer, maybe. Her hair and makeup were as impeccable as usual. She might have worn the lightweight blouse and skirt to work. He felt like he was on a date with a new and very intriguing woman.

Which was wrong.

Absolutely wrong.

She was his business partner. His friend of fifteen years. She bossed him around a lot. She hated frozen pizza for breakfast.

She was having four babies.

That was the deal-breaker for him.

"Does it feel different now that you know the gender of the babies?" The seemingly random question wasn't out of the blue. He'd been going at this all wrong—forcing himself to think only about business. What he had to do was focus on those kids—they'd knock this crazy attraction nonsense out cold.

"Yeah." Her lips were moist as she took another small bite of omelet, chewed. Joe watched her neck as she swallowed, wondering if it had gotten slimmer, longer, more vulnerable-looking with her pregnancy. "It seems more real."

To him, too. He'd just have to concentrate on that. Until fear of the changes the babies would bring to her life made him worry about her future with B&R. Then he'd concentrate on canoeing.

"I wonder if they're identical."

He stopped with a bite of grapefruit halfway to his mouth. "Four babies from the same egg?"

"No, two. I could be having two sets of identical twins."

"Is that common?"

"It's not uncommon, but there's more chance that they're fraternal."

"Could there be one set of identical twins and one set of fraternal?"

"Yep."

Kind of mind-boggling, all the possibilities. The dangers, risks, responsibilities…

"I'm off," he said, jumping up to dump the rest of his breakfast down the garbage disposal. "If you need anything lifted or moved, leave it and I'll do it tomorrow." He pulled his keys out of his pocket.

She was still at the table, eating, watching him. Her gray eyes were larger than he remembered, translucent and mysterious. Why did he so badly want to know the secrets they held?

"Don't wait dinner for me," he added, and walked swiftly to the door.

His Lexus was two miles down the road before he took an easy breath.

ON SUNDAY, EIGHT DAYS LATER, Elise was waiting for Joe in the family room when he came in the door from his basketball game.

"I hate to ask, but do you have an hour or so to go with me to look at a stroller?" They'd been pretty good at avoiding each other all week, and the few times they'd had dinner, had talked only about work or the changes the babies were going to make in her home life. "It's a used one on sale for seven hundred dollars," she continued, speaking of the stroller she'd found advertised in the paper that morning. "It's the first one for four I've found in the state and I'll have to take it today if I want it."

She was rambling and couldn't seem to stop. He looked so damned good standing there in a muscle shirt that showed more chest hair than it covered, while she'd had to let out the drawstring on the cotton capri pants she was wearing. "I'm not sure I can fit it into the Corvette, and it's going to be too heavy for me to lift." She stared at his shoes. "I'm sure the couple selling it will help me there, though."

"I'll take you."

"I can order one new, that they'd deliver, but I'm looking at twelve to fifteen hundred if I do that, and—"

"Elise." Joe put a finger on her lips. "I'm happy to go. Do I have time to shower first?"

Lips tingling from that touch, Elise nodded. And sat on the family room sofa to wait for him. Samantha was there. She could pet her. And it was the room in the house farthest from the bathroom where her business partner would be standing naked under running water.

"YOU'RE GOING TO HAVE TO do some serious training if you're ever going to push that thing." Joe's words, though teasing, struck fear in Elise's heart. They were standing in the driveway of the home of Merle and Abby Hudson, in Alto, Michigan.

"It's not that bad," Merle, a hefty man, said.

"We had four kids under the age of five and Abby did just fine."

Elise looked at Abby, who was about twice her size, then eyed the two sets of side-by-side seats. "Did you ever try one that had four seats in tandem?" she asked the friendly woman.

"Once." Abby laughed. "We rented one when we visited my mother. The thing was so long I couldn't steer it right, couldn't hold open a door and push through at the same time, and while I could see kids three and four, I had no idea what one and two were doing."

"Our three-year-old had managed to slide out of the safety straps, and Abby didn't know it until he stood up," Merle, dressed in overalls without a shirt, added.

That convinced her. Two sets of two it would be. She wrote the Hudsons a check, watched while they showed her how to fold the contraption for travel, and stepped back as Merle and Joe loaded it into the back of Joe's Lexus.

"So, you're really having quads, huh?" Abby asked. Elise could see she was going to have to get used to people staring at her stomach. Or never go outside.

"Yeah, I really am." She resisted the urge to cover her protruding belly.

"How far along are you? Five, six months?"

"Fifteen weeks."

"So you've gained what, eight or nine pounds?"

"Close to twenty."

"Whew. What're the next three months going to bring?"

Elise tried to laugh. "Hopefully only about twenty more. I've been told I'm not going to be able to see my feet for at least eight weeks. And might not be able to walk much, if at all, at the end."

"Well, hey, give me a call if you need to gripe or anything," the friendly young woman said. As Joe closed the trunk of his car, Merle approached. "Is this you two's first time around?" Merle looked back and forth between Elise and Joe, who was walking toward them now.

Elise frowned.

"Your first pregnancy he means," Abby added.

Mortified, Elise couldn't look at Joe. "Oh… I'm—"

"Yeah, first time," Joe piped up. "And so far, it's smooth sailing. Thanks so much for the stroller. We really appreciate it. And now, we've got to get going—more shopping to do, you know…"

With another couple of innocuously friendly comments, Joe got them out of there—without having given up Elise's phone number.

"I'M SORRY." Elise wasn't sure if she was suffering from morning sickness or was just sick at heart. The sun was too hot. The risks too great. Optimism seemed pointless.

Joe glanced from the road to her and back. "For what?"

"Back there," she said, staring at the license plate of the pickup in front of them. B 4 U. "Putting you in that mess."

"We bought a stroller. No big deal."

"It should have occurred to me that asking you to do things with me would put you in an awkward position. The more I'm showing the more people are going to assume you're the babies' father."

"You know that old saying about assuming, don't you?"

"I can't remember it."

"When you assume something you make an ass out of you and me."

Between him and the guy in front of them, she was surrounded by jokesters.

At least Joe didn't sound nearly as upset as she'd thought he'd be. As he had a right to be.

"I'll be more careful in the future," she assured him, anyway.

"You've got real things to worry about, Elise," he said, his voice sobering. "Don't make them up where they don't exist. What do I care what a couple of perfect strangers think? Or what anyone thinks? People who know me know the truth. And it's not like being the father of your babies would be a bad thing. For any guy who wanted kids, that is."

He had such a way with words.

Her heart, instead of feeling lighter, sank, which

made no sense at all. She sat there next to him, growing fatter by the second, feeling like she had a disease and he'd rather die than catch it.

"In any case, thanks for coming to my rescue."

"That's my job."

And to him that's all this was, Elise knew. To her, too. She'd just lost sight of that for a moment or two.

"People are bound to be curious, you know," he added as they took I-96 into Grand Rapids.

"Not that many of us know someone personally who's had quadruplets," he added.

"I didn't plan to be one of them." Elise laid her head against the seat back. "The plan was to have a quiet, normal pregnancy and create a strong and loving home for my baby."

"You know what they say about the best-laid plans."

"Yes, Joe, I know that one." Elise chuckled. It was hard to stay completely blue around Joe.

"Folks are going to want to know about the father, too," he said gently. "How a guy handles the advent of four babies at once. How he's going to support them. How he feels about middle-of-the-night feedings and changing diapers."

She knew what Joe's answers would be.

"And when they find out that I'm doing this on my own," she said, "they're going to look at me like I'm certifiable."

"Since when have you cared what other people think?"

Since always. Why did he think she'd worked so hard to create a new life for herself? To hide her past? Because she couldn't bear the pity on others' faces when they heard the truth. Couldn't stand to be set apart as different. Hated the thought of them looking at her and wondering what she might really have looked like if fate—and Thomas Fuller—hadn't stepped in.

"I don't," she said and wished it were true.

"SINCE WE'RE OUT, what do you say we drive into Grand Rapids and hit a couple of car lots?"

Just the way she'd envisioned her Sunday afternoon—walking around on black pavement in the hot sun staring at cars. "Sure," she said. If Joe wanted to see cars, they'd see cars. He was sacrificing almost six months of his life for her. She could give him an afternoon.

"WHAT ELSE IS BOTHERING YOU?" Joe had racked his brain for something to explain Elise's mood. He'd never seen her like this before, wondered if it was a product of the pregnancy, or just his seeing her in a more personal light. Everyone had bad days, bad moods, down times. Most managed to cover them up, at least to a point, while at work.

"I'm fine."

"This is me, Elise," he said as they drove

between tall areas of woods interspersed with patches of green grass. "I might have missed some things about you over the years, but I do know when you're bothered."

"You're going to think I'm whining."

"You have every right to whine."

"I asked for this, brought it on myself."

"You asked for one, got four. You were instrumental in the process, but you aren't fate, my dear."

"Why are we going to a car lot?" She glanced around the car. "You just bought this less than a year ago. It's nice."

He was glad she liked it. "In case you missed it, that Corvette of yours isn't going to hold two car seats, let alone four."

"Oh."

She looked so pathetic he almost laughed— except that he knew she wasn't faking it. For whatever reason, today Elise was having a hard time with everything.

He wished to God he knew what to do about it.

Going canoeing probably wasn't going to do it. And probably neither had running off to play basketball that morning. Maybe she was spending too much time alone for someone who was facing major and very frightening change.

He tried to enjoy the scenery they passed, the blue sky and familiar roads. And tried not to panic as he felt the chains of her needs tightening around him.

It was only for five more months. A blip in the span of a lifetime.

"So what, besides your car, has you down?" he asked again five minutes of silence later. They were still a few miles from the city, and he couldn't stand to see her so unhappy.

"I only have two arms."

Was she serious? She was staring straight ahead, no teasing smile in sight.

"Most of us do."

"But most of us aren't going to have four babies that need to be held. Think about it, Joe. No matter what I do I won't be able to care for my own children by myself."

He recognized the panic in her voice. He fought panic, too, every time he thought about her leaving B&R. Or being unable to return.

"Of course you will, if you need to." His switch to salesman mode was automatic, a defense mechanism because he couldn't afford to fail. "There'll be a lot of repetition, but you'll keep a schedule, do two at once if you can manage. Say a feeding is at one." He drove on, winging it as he went, drawing from the vast experience he'd gained growing up with six siblings. "It'll take about two minutes per baby, one when you get really good at it, to change diapers. That's four minutes. Half an hour at the most for feeding—should be able to get that down to about fifteen minutes, assuming they're eating well. That's thirty-four minutes. You get the other two up, repeat the process, and have an hour to sleep before the three o'clock feeding rolls around."

The frown on her face wasn't promising.

"That'll only be for the first few weeks," he assured her. "Maybe a couple of months at most and then they start sleeping longer. Once you get them on cereal, they'll sleep through the night."

"And if all four are crying at once?"

"You buy earplugs, tend to them one at a time, and life goes on."

"But—"

"You ever hear of a baby dying from crying?"

"No."

"And the best news is," he said, pulling onto Twenty-eighth Street, "you aren't going to be doing it all alone. I'll be there for the first week or so, depending on when you deliver, and then it'll be the first of the year and your salary will increase and you'll be able to hire someone to help out for another six weeks until they sleep through the night, at which time you'll only need daytime care."

"You're planning to help with nighttime feedings?"

"You going to be able to think about B&R if you get no sleep?"

"No."

"Then I'll be helping."

"You hate anything to do with babies."

"Doesn't mean I'm not good at it. Ask my mother. She'll vouch for me. So will the four of my six siblings I fed and diapered."

"You'd do that for me?" Her mouth was almost hanging open.

Of course he would. Didn't she know that by now?

"I'd do it for B&R," he said.

Nodding, she continued to stare at him as he pulled gratefully into the parking lot of the dealership he'd just noticed.

"So, what kind of minivan do you want?"

SHE WAS NOW the proud almost-owner of a new Buick Terraza seven-passenger minivan with all-season blackwall tires, four-wheel antilock brakes, a latch system that included lower anchors and top tethers for children and, also, at Joe's insistence, a built-in DVD player that would be suspended from the ceiling of the car and viewed from all four car seats. The van would be ready for delivery Tuesday night.

She was too tired to mourn the impending loss of her Corvette—she was trading it in as part of the deal—as she sat at the kitchen table, having a glass of milk before bed that night. Brochures for the van were spread out on the table before her. She wasn't looking at them.

"Buyer's remorse?" Joe asked, coming in from the garage. He'd run home to collect his mail and another suitcase of clothes.

"Business partner's gratitude," she told him honestly. "I'd have gotten around to the idea that I had to lose the 'Vette eventually, but I hadn't been ready to consider it yet. You made it all relatively painless. Thank you."

She expected a quip back. His quiet, "You're welcome," surprised her.

As did his next move. He pulled out a chair and sat down.

"I think we should amend our plan a bit."

She started to shake. "Okay."

He was leaving.

She didn't blame him.

What in hell am I going to do now? She'd thought, lying burned and orphaned in a hospital, she'd experienced her life's share of helplessness.

She hadn't.

"We need to get out a little more," he said, his eyes serious as, hands clasped together on the table, he leaned toward her.

Those same hands had helped her up into the van that afternoon when she'd almost lost her balance. They'd held her around her thickening waist until she'd regained her equilibrium. And been there to help her back down again when their test drive was through.

She could still remember their warmth through her blouse.

And how much she'd liked having them there.

"Why?" she asked when she realized he was

waiting for her to say something. She thought she knew the answer. He was really telling her that *he* had to get out more, because soon he wasn't going to be living here. He knew she'd been having an inappropriate feeling or two about him.

"I'm going to say something you probably aren't going to like. I want you to hear me out and not get all defensive."

Oh, God. It was worse than she'd thought.

CHAPTER NINE

"OKAY." Elise braced herself. She'd lived through some excruciatingly hard times. She could handle whatever Joe had to dish out.

"I don't think it's good for you to be alone so much right now," he said quickly.

She immediately began to form a denial, which he gave her no chance to utter.

"I know you like your independence, and I understand that, but right now, with so much going on, so much uncertainty and worry, all this time alone probably isn't such a good thing."

What did this have to do with his leaving?

"What are you proposing?" she asked, needing him to quit humoring her and just get to it.

"That, unless you have plans with someone else, we eat together at least five nights a week and at least twice on weekends—whether breakfast, lunch or supper. And we go out for dinner at least once a week. I'd like to suggest, as a caveat, though this part is up for discussion, that we also see one movie a week outside the house."

"What?"

"What do you mean, what?"

"You want us to eat together more."

"Right."

"Here."

"Yes. And out at least once a week." He sounded as though he were explaining something simple to a child.

"You'll still be staying here at night?"

"Of course." His frown wasn't as nice as his humoring compassion had been. "We made a deal. Why would you ask that?"

Because I thought about you naked in the shower. She threw up her hand. "It's been a rough day. I wouldn't blame you for rethinking things, is all."

"Do you get to rethink them?"

Not hardly. She was already pregnant. "No."

"Then why would you think *I* can?"

She could give him several reasons, but was half-afraid he hadn't thought of them. Why give him cause to go if he didn't think he had to?

"That's all you wanted? The whole dinner thing?"

"Yes."

She should argue. She knew that. She shouldn't consume so much of his life. It wasn't good for either of them.

"Okay."

He sat back. "That's it? Just okay? No argument?"

"Are you prepared to listen to anything I have to say on the matter?"

"No."

"I didn't think so."

"It's settled then. Good."

She sipped her milk, avoiding his gaze.

"Why haven't you ever been this agreeable at work?" His voice had a teasing tone.

"Because I can afford to have you mad at me, there."

MONDAY NIGHT over a slowly prepared dinner of risotto carbonara, Elise resisted the urge to prop her swelling feet on the seat across from her. No reason to have Joe worrying—or hassling her—about something that, while irritating and uncomfortable, was completely natural to her condition.

She was pregnant. There was bound to be discomfort. Joe would have her staying home from work, and that she wasn't about to do. Not unless her babies' lives were in danger.

She'd brought the little television in from the converted nursery and put it on the kitchen counter so they could watch television while they ate. And not have to talk.

Joe was engrossed in the news. She'd heard all she needed to know.

"Talking about the feeding schedule, are you planning to breast-feed?"

The rice on her fork slid to her plate. "Who was talking about a feeding schedule?" she asked around the glass she raised to her lips to hide behind.

"*We* were." He pushed some rice around on his plate, stabbed a piece of ham, scooped up some peas, seemed to thoroughly enjoy the bite he'd made. "Yesterday."

"Oh. Right."

Elise got up and carried her plate to the sink, rinsed it and put it in the dishwasher, looked around for something else to do.

"So, are you?"

Turning, she leaned against the counter, folding her arms on top of the stomach that seemed to be protruding another inch every day. "Yes."

"Good." He scooped up another bite.

"Why is that good?"

"It's generally considered to be healthier for the babies."

She eyed him critically. "Something else you learned during your youth?"

"Something I read about when I was waiting for you at the clinic the other day."

The man never ceased to amaze her. "Well, they do say it's healthier," she said. "Studies show that babies who are breast-fed tend to have fewer ear infections and other common childhood maladies."

"So how does that happen with four of them? Does your body know to give you that much milk?"

Elise moved her arms up a notch, half covering herself. She was standing in her kitchen talking to her partner about her breasts.

And he acted like they were loaves of bread.

She told him what she'd been told when she'd asked that very question six weeks before. "Mothers produce milk based on need. The more the babies take, the more I'll produce. But in the case of four of them, I'm probably going to need to pump and also supplement with formula."

"Ohhh," he said, nodding his head as though she'd cleared up some burning issue for him.

He'd been worried about the work her breasts were going to be required to do? Thinking about them at all?

Noticing them?

Of course, Joe was a man. Men noticed breasts. But Joe? Looking at hers? The idea was…was…

She didn't know what it was. Nor did she like how the thought made her feel—as though she wanted him to like her breasts. Enough to want to touch them.

Must be her hormones. And the fact that she was beginning to feel like an unattractive, overweight piece of machinery.

He was still nodding. Chewing. The TV droning softly.

"What?" she finally asked, though she was pretty sure she should have followed her instincts and left the room instead.

"I was just trying to figure out how you could breast-feed, which is best for the babies, and have someone help you with feeding times. I hadn't considered the pump idea—wasn't sure how that would work with feedings every two hours. But if you're going to be supplementing with formula, anyway, whoever is helping will be able to do those bottles."

Joe seemed to be spending a lot of time lately thinking about her personal life. More time than he'd spent, collectively, in fifteen years, she'd wager.

She kind of liked that.

And hated that she felt that way. It was only going to hurt her in the end.

Because it *would* end. She knew that without a doubt. Joe had lost the love of his life because he couldn't get over his anxiety at the thought of children in his home, needing things he couldn't provide, creating chaos he couldn't control. Elise ought to know. She'd nursed many a cocktail with him as he dealt with the angst of watching his marriage die over something he couldn't seem to change.

If Kelly hadn't been enough to keep him around for one baby, Elise sure as hell wouldn't be with four.

JOE STUMBLED OUT OF BED at his usual time Friday morning, heading for the bathroom instead of an extra few minutes' snooze in the kitchen while his coffee brewed. He had a breakfast meeting with Michigan Local Banks that morning and would be sure to get his daily supply of caffeine there.

The peaceful quiet of the well-kept old house wrapped around him. He liked these times in the morning after Elise left for work. Alone, but not alone.

Eyes still half closed, he made it through the dining room to the hall without stubbing his toe, divesting himself of the T-shirt he'd been wearing to bed only since he'd lived here. He hopped and stepped out of his shorts, as well, intending to drop them both in his side of the laundry receptacle behind the bathroom door.

His underwear would follow as soon as he'd shaved. In that Joe was a creature of habit. Shave first, then shower. No matter what they said about warm, wet skin making for an easier shave. It was also, in his experience, a less-close one.

He reached for the bathroom door and knocked into warm flesh instead.

"Oh!"

Joe's eyes opened wide as his hands grabbed instinctively, catching Elise by the sides to steady her. And himself. His T-shirt and shorts fell to the floor.

"I thought you were gone."

In a sleeveless shift and sandals, she was obviously ready for work. "I'm late. The babies weren't real cooperative this morning."

He meant to drop his hands, but studied her color instead. "Maybe you should stay home."

"No." She wasn't moving. At all. "I'm fine now."

Elise's gaze dropped, and then rose again—to about his chest. He waited for her to pull away. To do something, since he obviously wasn't doing so.

"You're always in the kitchen sleeping right now."

God, she was exquisite. Her gray eyes huge, luminous, her mouth trembling, moist, inviting. How could he have missed seeing this before?

"Breakfast meeting. Too much caffeine." He hoped the response was pertinent to whatever she'd said.

She didn't seem to find anything wrong with it. Didn't object to it.

She licked her lips. He noticed. And kept noticing them. They looked so soft, so open.

They seemed to be calling to him. Joe lowered his head an inch. Stopped. Studied those lips some more. They didn't move away. If anything they seemed to move toward him.

He lowered his head a little more, cautiously reaching for something, and touched his mouth to hers. Tentatively. Testing. Needing to know.

It wasn't a kiss, not really. His nerves were jumping, urging him to do more, take them someplace else, discover what was just out of his grasp.

Suddenly aware of Elise's warmth coming through his fingers, his palms, as they kept contact with her sides, Joe pulled and she came closer, her dress touching his bare legs, enflaming him. And he covered her mouth completely.

A kiss had never been so much. She tasted cool, of toothpaste, and smelled like flowers. He recognized the scent. He showered with it wafting around him every morning. And her tongue was hot, bold, giving him a response he didn't recognize as Elise at all.

Arms around her now, her breasts against his bare chest, he found her buttocks with both hands and pressed her against him.

And felt the hardness of her belly, a wedge between them, stopping him cold.

Joe froze for a moment, with no idea how to end the moment.

As it turned out, he didn't have to. Elise pulled away, stepped around him and into her room, closing her door behind her.

Staring at the door, he knew he should knock. Speak with her. Apologize.

Set things straight between them.

And he had absolutely nothing to say. Not to her. Not to himself.

With a silent curse, Joe entered the bathroom, closing the door firmly behind him, and turned on the shower.

Today shaving would have to wait.

AT HER DESK Friday morning, Elise dropped her pencil and stared at her stomach. Had that been a baby moving? The sensation had come and gone so fast she couldn't be sure. But she was fairly certain she'd never felt that little bubble-pop sensation before in her life.

She held her breath, waiting for it to come again.

Glancing out her window to see who was around, she wanted to call out to someone to come witness the miracle going on in her office. But didn't want to risk shocking her children into stillness.

If, indeed, any of them were moving at all.

They all had the right number of arms and legs. She'd seen them. But with the babies measuring not much more than two inches apiece, those tiny limbs might not be strong enough to move with enough force to get through the placenta to her nerve endings.

Elise giggled. What normal mother sat around analyzing body parts at a time like this?

She glanced at her phone, the inner office line. She wanted to call Joe.

And couldn't.

Then the phone started to ring. But no lights were blinking.

Another ring and Elise blinked, focused. Someone was calling her cell phone. Was it Joe? Ready to speak to her again?

Was she ever going to be ready to speak to him? To face him?

"Hello?" She grabbed it on the third ring.

"Elise Richardson?"

The voice was female. And unfamiliar.

"This is Elise."

"Ms. Richardson? This is Joyce Merritt, director of the Bonder Fertility Center."

Why were they calling her? She'd paid her bill in full.

"I…um…have an unusual situation here…"

Something was wrong with her babies. Genetically. And they knew about it. They'd used the wrong sperm, one with abnormalities that should have been disposed of. Elise's thoughts tripped over themselves, racing to one fear after another, each topping the one before it. Could a clinic recall kids? Force her to terminate her pregnancy?

"What?" she managed when the other woman left her last sentence hanging. *Just tell me, dammit. And I'll deal with it. Whatever it is.*

"Your agreement with us was a bit out of the ordinary," Ms. Merrit said slowly, almost defensively.

"It's legally binding, agreed upon by your lawyers."

"Yes, I know. We aren't questioning that. We just don't have a policy to govern certain issues—paternal issues."

"This has to do with my babies' father?"

"Yes."

"You know which of the five men fathered them?"

"No," the woman said. "At least, I don't. And neither does anyone else here. A choice was made, the appropriate number assigned to the choice was recorded, but no one looked up the name. And those records are sealed, according to your agreement."

Which meant she got the right specimen, didn't it? Elise rubbed her belly, breathing a little easier. The babies were fine. That was the main thing.

"So what's the problem?"

"According to your contract, the five potential fathers were all granted the right to seek out knowledge of any resulting children when said children reach adult status."

"Correct." A provision provided because it was usual practice.

"Prior to that, the fathers can seek knowledge only with the permission of you, the mother, through us."

She knew all of this.

"And that's why I'm calling," Joyce Merritt said, speaking more quickly now. "One of the five men you brought to us as donors has requested the right to buy back his sperm, if indeed he was one of the four unused. If he *was* used, he'd like contact with you and the resulting child. Or children."

The clinic knew she was having quads.

"Five months ago all five men swore they had no interest in contact."

"This man has since contracted mumps, which left him sterile."

Elise felt the news, the blow, as though it were her own. "Was he married?" Suddenly the question she hadn't asked mattered.

"His wife was killed in a car accident last year."

Elise's heart opened with compassion—and closed with defensiveness at the same time. She hated that another human being was suffering tragedy. And these babies were hers. She'd been very careful to establish the singleness of her own-ership—her parenthood—from the very beginning.

"With your permission, we can unseal the records and find out if he is, indeed, the father of your children."

"No." The answer was straight gut reaction.

"Then Mr. Fallow requests that we ask if you're willing to see him, speak with him. If nothing else he wants to make certain that you're taken care of, that you and any children resulting from your en-counter with us are provided for."

Elise sat still in her chair, staring at the hallway outside her door. Joe was right down that strip of carpet. Unless he was out.

"Adam Fallow is the one?"

"Yes."

She'd never met him in person, only seen a picture and communicated by phone and e-mail.

"You don't have to have anything to do with this, Ms. Richardson," Joyce Merritt added, her voice not without sympathy. "I'm just under obli-gation to relay the request."

"I understand."

Far more than she wanted to. What if *her* only chance to have children of her own had been given away to someone else? It would be another kind of death. Suffered through and grieved as those she'd lost before.

Could she be so cruel as to willingly allow, in a sense, cause, that anguish for someone else?

And yet, if she did as this man asked, she'd be losing the very thing she most needed and wanted—her own family. Her children weren't even born yet, and already they'd be facing a life of split family, split home. She'd be facing times, holidays, without them.

Exactly what she'd prevented by hiring a very expensive attorney and signing the airtight document that had been created at her behest.

She could unseal the records. Find out if the man was the father. If he wasn't, they were home free. She wouldn't know who the father was. No one else would know. They'd only know that the number of the donor didn't match that of the now sterile man. He could have his sample and go on his way.

Or they'd find out that Adam Fallow *was* the father of her four babies. And everything she'd planned for, everything she wanted for her children, would be irrevocably changed. She didn't want the person who'd sold sperm to have a specific face and name. To stake a claim to her family.

He was a donor. That was all he'd wanted to be.

And what if he was a man who'd lost the chance to ever father children of his own?

"I'll see him."

CHAPTER TEN

JOE TOOK A PASS on the weekly staff lunch. He met
Melanie at a popular eatery in Grand Rapids
instead. And made a point of kissing her goodbye
when they parted at her car an hour later. They
weren't exclusive. Melanie saw other men and he
saw other women. He just needed to get his kisses
back where they belonged—which was anywhere
away from his partner.

And then he got his butt back to the office.

"I need information by this afternoon detailing
the software integration necessary to bring Michigan Local Banks onboard," he greeted Elise from
her office doorway immediately upon his return.

"I'll have Mark and Colby get right on it," she
said, naming their chief financial officer and
resident computer guru with barely a glance in
Joe's direction. "And could you make a call re-
garding the employee packets on the new child
care group? They want their first payroll to run
next Friday and we're missing more than we have."

"I'll do it right now." He turned to leave.

"I won't be home for dinner tonight," she said. Joe backed up, glanced at her bent head. He'd hoped this morning's episode was going to go away. That she'd be big enough to ignore the lapse and allow them to continue as though it had never happened.

It appeared they were going to have to talk about it.

"I'm meeting someone after work," she added.

Her head rose, her gaze on him for a split second, before it settled just over his left shoulder. Her mouth fell open.

Joe swung around at the same time that Angela spoke.

"Home for dinner?" she said, her mouth open. "You two are living together?" Angela's voice rose, finishing a squeal that could probably be heard on the floor below, let alone both ends of their suite.

"What?" Sam came around the corner. "Did Angela just say the two of you are shacking up?" With a huge grin, he nudged Joe. "Does this mean the babies are yours, after all?"

"No!" Joe thought fast. And came up with nothing. Except to stand in front of Elise's door, blocking her from the immediate view of their staff.

"My doctor would rather I not stay alone," Elise said, getting up and pushing past him to face the employees quickly filling the hall. "Joe has offered to stay at my house until I can make other arrangements."

She made it sound so temporary. But then, she wouldn't tell their staff that she was financially strapped. Nor would he have her do so.

"It's strictly business." Elise's tone was filled with such no-nonsense confidence, Joe believed her himself.

Which left him to wonder who she was meeting after work. And why he cared.

ADAM FALLOW WAS A NICE MAN. A good-looking nice man. In his midthirties, his light summer slacks, polo shirt and leather shoes giving him the air of a man who had the world at his fingertips. A man who could get what he wanted.

Elise debated walking away before she introduced herself.

"Mr. Fallow?" she asked instead, approaching the cement bench outside the busy restaurant in downtown Grand Rapids.

He stood immediately, the concern in his eyes the only sign that the man had suffered a day in his life. "Ms. Richardson?"

A couple passed between them and when they were gone, Adam was staring at her stomach. Elise wished again that she hadn't agreed to this meeting. She had an airtight contract. Owed Adam Fallow nothing.

"I'm Elise Richardson, yes."

The man looked her up and down, twice, his gaze finally coming to rest on her face. "Forgive me," he said then, shoving his hands in his pockets. "I didn't mean to stare. You're breathtakingly beautiful."

The discovery seemed to surprise him.

"Thank you."

Shaking his head, he chuckled and stared at his shoes for the time it took a family of five to pass by. "That was rude, too, wasn't it?" he asked. And then continued. "I'm sorry, I'm not handling this at all well. I just… I mean, a woman with your looks could have your pick of men…"

Elise's heart softened slightly as he dug himself in further. "It's okay," she broke in before he could completely bury himself. "If I'd heard about a woman choosing to have a baby as I did, I'd probably have expected her to be date-challenged, too."

"Well, yeah…I guess," he said, peering at her from under his brow. "I…" He stopped, rocked back on his heels. "Would you like to get something to eat?"

She was starving. And looking forward to splurging on a burger from Fuddruckers right down the street. Topping it off with one of their award-winning chocolate fudge brownies. Her one food extravagance for the duration of the pregnancy. Today she deserved the treat.

"Not tonight," she told Adam. "I don't think we should get to know each other any better until I

decide what I'm going to do next where you're concerned."

"Fair enough."

"You requested this meeting. What did you
want to say?"

"I'm not sure." His honesty was disarming. "I
just thought that if we met, face-to-face, we could
bring the human element back into all this."

Which was what she most wanted to avoid.

"The contract you signed is binding."

"I'm not disputing that." He stepped back
behind the bench and away from any further inter-
ruption from dinner-goers.

She joined him there. "But you're counting on
the emotional element to compel me to set it aside."

"I'm not counting on anything. But let's face it,
I have nothing left to lose. I figured that someone
who wanted children so badly that she'd go to all
the trouble you did to have them, would understand what I'm facing."

"I do understand."

"But?"

It was Elise's turn to look away—at the busy street,
the traffic whizzing by several yards in front of them.
She wondered what Joe was doing for dinner—if
he'd gone home and put a frozen pizza in the oven.

How she wished she could be there with him,
safely ensconced in her isolated little world.

A world that, as of this morning, was no longer
safe at all.

"I don't know," she told the man in front of her, giving him the one thing she could give him. Her honesty. "What you're asking could affect the rest of my life, and the lives of my children."

"Children?" He glanced down again. "There's more than one?"

She didn't want to tell him there were four—as though that meant there were plenty to go around. These were siblings, family, not commodities.

Elise nodded.

And hated the light she saw in his eyes. Interest. Enthusiasm. Caring.

A complete antithesis of the horror that had filled Joe's expression when he'd heard her news.

To Adam's credit he didn't say another word.

"No matter what I decide, you'll need to understand that I have no intention of splitting up my family," she told him then.

He nodded.

"Give me a week."

His shoulders slumped as his gaze met hers directly, his eyes moist, though not brimming. "Thank you."

"I may decide to deny your request."

"You're thinking about it. That's enough for now," he told her. His smile looked genuine. "I'm an inventor," he said. "I needed the money for—"

"Stop." Elise held up one hand. "I won't be subject to emotional manipulation."

At least no more than she could help.

JOE MADE A COUPLE OF phone calls, looking for a dinner date. And when he realized he was phoning women he knew were either busy on Friday nights, moved away or newly attached, he quit kidding himself and drove through a fast-food joint for a bag of dinner, took it to his condominium, flipped on the television and settled in.

Accepting that he wasn't going to be around all summer, he'd turned off the air-conditioning two weeks before and his luxury condo had to be pushing eighty-five degrees. One hamburger out of the way and he had perspiration rolling down his temples. He sucked on his soda straw.

But the television was good. He could watch news to his heart's content.

And sweat.

The second hamburger was all he got through before stuffing the rest of the fries and dessert in the trash. He sucked on his soda straw again and came up empty.

How fitting, he thought. He'd been thinking about Elise since she'd left the office an hour before. Imagining who she might be with—and why. Just as he'd called Melanie for lunch, had Elise called an old boyfriend? Was she going to kiss him just to wipe away the taste and feel of Joe from her lips?

He had no answers.

TV off, Joe was back out in the Lexus fifteen minutes after he'd pulled it into his garage. He might as well think in comfort. And be there when she got home.

SHE DIDN'T LOOK like she'd had a great time. Bending over the kitchen faucet, in the process of changing the washer, Joe caught a glimpse of her from under his elbow. Her face was pale, drawn, her hair flat, as though she'd been driving with the window open.

"I brought you a brownie."

From Fuddruckers, according to the bag she'd put on the counter. Much better than the fried-pie thing he'd thrown in the Dumpster back at his condo. "Thanks."

And if that's where she'd been to dinner, her excursion hadn't been anything like the hot date he'd been envisioning. Darin sat on the counter beside him, watching her.

"I'm tired. I think I'll turn in."

At eight o'clock? Without telling him where she'd been?

She took her cat and Joe grabbed the wrench he'd borrowed from the tool bench in her garage. "Sleep well."

He supposed she did. Even though he lay awake for hours, he didn't hear anything from her room the rest of the night.

ELISE WAS SITTING at the kitchen table when Joe came out the next morning. Already showered and dressed in a denim jumper, she sat empty-handed, just staring. Her cats were nowhere in sight.

"What's up?"

"Good morning." She stood, grabbed some eggs

from the refrigerator. "Would you like an omelet? It sounds good to me, but I can't eat a whole one."

As though omelets came in one size only? As though omelets were what she'd been sitting there thinking about?

"Sure. Can I have ten minutes to jump in the shower first?" And put on something besides his sleep shorts and T-shirt?

Her affirmative reply followed him back through the dining room.

FIFTEEN MINUTES LATER, Joe felt more up to facing his partner/friend/housemate. It was Saturday. His sacred free time. He'd already put on his running shoes with denim shorts and a T-shirt in preparation for that canoe trip down the river he'd been meaning to take.

Today was definitely the day.

Elise had the television on—a shopping channel Kelly had had a running monthly account with. As he watched her from the doorway and then jumped in to help with the toast and setting the table, Joe felt pretty confident that any danger of him making a huge mistake—like finding Elise sexually desirable—was long gone. All he had to do was look at her protruding stomach.

Not that he didn't find the mound appealing in itself. Sexy even. But it was caused by babies.

And they made Joe run in the other direction every time. His loss of Kelly was all the proof he needed.

"THAT WAS GOOD." They were the first words they'd spoken since her "pass the jelly, please" when they'd first sat down. "Thank you," Joe tacked on for good measure.

"You're welcome."

He wiped his mouth. Put his napkin on his plate. Time to put his stuff in the dishwasher and go. The river was waiting.

"You going to tell me what's troubling you?" He hadn't quite stood yet. But he would. Just as soon as she answered him.

It had to be the kiss. And he could quickly put that fear to rest for her. They were going to be fine. Back to normal already.

"I had a call from the Bonder Fertility Clinic yesterday."

Joe frowned. "Is something wrong?"

Her shrug wasn't all that reassuring. Setting down her fork on a half-eaten omelet, she covered her stomach with her arms. He'd seen her do that a few times before, usually when she was upset.

"One of the donors wants to know if he's the father."

The statement was so out of the blue, Joe sat back. Shocked. "Well, he can't. You have a contract. What's done is done."

"It's not that easy."

"Of course it is!" He'd right this immediately. "From everything you've told me, you very carefully planned this whole thing," he reminded her. "The man has no legal rights whatsoever."

"I know."

"Then what's the problem?" And why was his blood pressure rising over this?

"He's since become sterile. The specimen he sold to me is his only chance of ever fathering children."

"That's garbage."

Elise's sad smile alerted Joe to the way he was sounding. Like someone who had a stake in any of this. Leaning his elbows on the table, he determined to correct the impression.

"I'm just thinking of you," he told her. "You've lost so much, worked so hard. You've been very careful, did everything the right way…"

"Yeah."

"So…"

Fiddling with a corner of her napkin, Elise frowned, looking at him as though he had some elusive piece of wisdom she couldn't find.

He didn't even have his wits about him, let alone any wisdom. He was too busy thinking about finding this guy and giving him a piece of his mind.

"Sometimes fate steps in. Tragedy happens," she said softly. "Adam lost his wife in a car accident last year."

So it was Adam now. Joe turned cold as a sinking suspicion set firmly in his gut. Was this Elise's mysterious appointment? Had she actually met the guy?

"What's that got to do with you?" he asked, aware of the lack of compassion he was showing toward this unknown man. "And anyway, that would have been *before* he answered your ad." So had no bearing on the situation—unless the son of a bitch was using the information to somehow manipulate Elise.

"I'm going to call my father," he said next. The man might have sired too many children in Joe's humble opinion, but he'd been a top-rate family lawyer for more than thirty years.

"I don't need a lawyer, Joe. At least not yet."

He disagreed. "If this guy even thinks he's going to blackmail you—"

"Adam has been a model of decorum." Instead of calming him, her words only infuriated Joe further.

Crossing his arms, he decided to keep his own counsel until he heard the entire story. Until he could figure out what was the matter with him. And figure out how to help her.

"So what's he want, exactly?"

"For me to unseal the records and find out if his sperm was the one of the five that was used."

"Why? So he can come after you for a share in the results?"

Joe heard the words coming out of his mouth and managed to feel some shame. He should have stayed in bed.

"Because if it wasn't his, he wants to purchase it back from me."

"Oh." He took a sip of cold coffee. "That's not

so bad, is it?" He met her gaze, struck again by the depths of mystery in her eyes. "It's not like you need it anymore."

"If the babies aren't his, that's exactly right," she said slowly. And then her face crumpled, her eyes filling with tears. "But what if he *is,* Joe? What if I agree to this and find out that he's the father? How will I ever be able to tell this man he can't have access to the only biological children he'll ever have?"

Joe started to hate the guy again.

Clasping his hands so they wouldn't betray him—he wanted to reach for her, pull her in his arms to offer the comfort that seemed to surface so naturally in him—Joe wished he knew what to say.

"So don't do it." He fell far short of what he'd hoped to achieve there.

She nodded, as though she'd already reached the decision herself, and Joe breathed a sigh of relief. She'd needed validation. He'd given it to her.

He could go canoeing now.

"But what if he isn't the father?" she said softly. "What if his sperm is sitting in a vault in Grand Rapids, his future biological children that will never be, simply because I'm too selfish to let him find out if they're there?"

"How'd this guy become sterile all of a sudden?" Joe was going from bad to worse. "Some injury?"

"He got the mumps."

Really. Joe had no idea adults really got that anymore. Or that it could actually cause sterility. Adjusting his butt in the chair, he considered his own virility from a different perspective than ever before.

Yeah, he didn't want kids in the worst way. But to think that his option to do so, his *ability* to do so could be compromised so easily…

"Joyce Merritt, the director of the clinic, told me yesterday when she called that with the swelling, something gets blocked and…"

A diet commercial was on—expostulating over all the food that could be eaten with continued weight loss if one only joined their system. Someone lost forty-two pounds in four months. Another woman lost her baby fat. Eating chocolate.

"…sometimes even an infection can cause…"

Joe shifted in his seat some more. Heard about a woman who felt sexy again now that she was thinner than she'd ever been in her life.

He wasn't sure the diet plan was such a great idea. It sounded too good to be true. But at least he was no longer fighting the urge to strangle some guy he'd never met. Or caring about his own fertility.

The commercial was over. Elise was looking at him expectantly.

"So what are you going to do?" he asked, hoping she wasn't waiting for some response to a question he hadn't heard.

"I don't know. I told him I'd get back to him in a week."

"So you spoke to him."

"He was my appointment after work."

He'd guessed right. But it was nothing to do with him.

"He took you to Fuddruckers?"

"*I* took me to Fuddruckers. I spent two minutes with him."

She went to dinner alone. Had one of the world's best hamburgers. Thinking of the bag of grease he'd thrown away the night before, Joe thought it a shame she hadn't asked him along.

"You must be considering this since you met with him."

"I have to consider it, don't I? Otherwise I'm arbitrarily making a decision that might go against my principles."

"You know it'll be much harder to say no now that you've met him, don't you?"

"Yes, but…I don't know, Joe. I know what it's like to lose loved ones. Maybe I thought he'd be a jerk and my conscience would be clear when I denied his request."

"There are many ways of being a jerk," Joe quickly pointed out. "Playing on your emotions, being charming only to get someone to do what you want—"

"I've already thought of that," she interrupted him. "But Adam wasn't any of those things. Truly.

Anyway, I think maybe what I'm going to do is meet with him one more time. Listen to what he has to say. Maybe there will be something there that will make my decision clear to me."

"I don't like that one bit." The words were said with far too much force. Probably because he was itchy to get out on the water.

"Why not?"

"What if the guy's a lunatic?"

"I'll meet him in a public place before dark and not walk to my car alone afterward. Besides, I had a thorough background check done on him, remember?"

Just like Elise to have all the answers.

So maybe she could answer this. Why did Joe, who had no vested interest in these children at all, who actually would benefit greatly if someone took over his job here for him and let him get back to the business of running a business with Elise, feel so threatened at the idea of Elise trotting off to meet with a man who may or may not have fathered her children?

Maybe she could provide an answer.

If he asked her.

Joe did not.

CHAPTER ELEVEN

ELISE HAD PLANNED to have dinner made before Joe got back from the river—and to have already eaten hers. And then Samantha decided to explore the inside of the washing machine when Elise left the lid open—with the appliance filling—to go collect the shorts and nightshirt she'd shoved under her pillow that morning. Samantha hadn't suffered any serious damage from the gushing water or suds, but she'd cut her head trying to spring out of there. Elise had spent most of the afternoon at the vet's office with an extremely stressed-out and headachy feline.

And that was why she'd ended up sitting across from her reluctant and far-too-sexy-for-her-good housemate at one of the round, umbrellaed tables on the back patio of the Flat River Grill, watching the ducks on the water and trying not to notice that the man had shoulders. Seriously broad shoulders.

He'd always had them. She just hadn't noticed before. Probably because she'd never had pregnancy hormones shooting through her body.

Or doubts and uncertainties climbing so high inside her she was in danger of choking on them.

She got through half of her cedar-smoked salmon and steamed red-skinned potatoes, managing to make only mildly derogatory comments about his pizza al forno Americana with pepperoni, sausage, red onion, mushrooms, green peppers, sauce and cheese. A fine seafood menu, and the man chose pizza.

And by then she was also finished telling him about Samantha's mild concussion, lack of stitches and good prognosis. The rest of the meal was spent discussing business.

"You don't have to do this, you know," Elise told Joe as she was strapping herself back into the front seat of his Lexus. "Have dinner with me most nights and take me out for dinner at least once. I appreciate the sentiment and, for that matter, your incredible friendship, but you're already going far beyond the call of duty by just staying at the house, Joe. I feel terrible taking up your social time, too."

She also felt terrible that she was ogling him as though he were any man on the street. Considering their fifteen-year partnership and the boundaries they'd successfully established, her unexpected sexual desire for him was entirely inappropriate. And dangerous.

Her feelings threatened the trust they'd built. If they lost that trust, they lost everything.

"If I don't feel terrible about it, why should you?" His shrug was as easy as the perplexed look he sent her.

But then, he didn't know that that shrug had just sent a thrill up her spine, or that, at dinner, for one second there she'd actually imagined those shoulders above her…

"Because I'm taking advantage of you," she said, "and eventually you'll start to resent me for it."

"You seem to have reframed reality, my dear," he said, starting the ignition and adjusting the air vents. "As I recall, I forced myself on you and then insisted that we eat dinner together. Frankly I did it all for purely selfish reasons."

The cold air was blissful in the hot car. "You did?"

"Of course I did. I can't run B&R without you. You are an asset, a commodity, and I'm merely protecting my investment."

If she hadn't known him for almost half her life, Elise might have taken offense at his repeated protestations that he was doing it all for B&R. But instead, his words pretty much calmed the panic that had been steadily growing in her since Friday morning and the kiss they would never, ever speak about.

Pretty much, but not entirely. There was something she had to call him on.

"You've got that intense note in your tone, Joe. The one you get when you're trying to convince someone of something—most often when you're trying to convince yourself that you mean what you're saying."

"I don't know what you're talking about." He seemed unusually interested in the summer strollers passing by on the sidewalk.

"It's the same tone, incidentally, that you had that Saturday when you dropped by and found me with an unpleasant bout of morning sickness."

"Passing out sick, and looking half-dead, you mean."

"Don't turn this on me."

Joe swiveled to face her, took a breath as though preparing a comeback and lifted a hand to her hair instead, brushing his fingers through it. "Let's not fight, Elise. You have a lot of things to think about right now, plans to make. I'm here because, all things considered, I want to be. Let's just leave it at that, okay?"

"O…ohhhhh." She'd meant to agree and stared at him, wide-eyed, instead.

"What?" He frowned, glanced down at her stomach. "Is something wrong?"

"Uh-uh." Elise shook her head. "I…think…someone just moved in there." She ought to know; she wasn't moving an inch.

An uncomfortable look crossed his face. And then she read interest in his eyes. Soon followed by caution.

"I thought it might have happened yesterday,"

she said, "but it came and went so fast. And never came back."

"It's probably just indigestion," he said, watching her. "You're only four months along. That's still too soon, isn't it?"

"Not with quads. Look at my stomach, Joe! I'm already really showing and that doesn't usually happen at four months, either."

Elise felt herself blushing when he did as she asked. And cursed herself for forgetting to watch her words. And then she forgot everything.

"There it is again!" she cried, grinning, feeling idiotically close to tears. "I'm sure that's a baby moving. I've never felt anything like it before!"

She covered the side of her belly with her hand. "Mama's here, little one," she said softly, choked up with this proof that her small family was growing inside of her. That her dreams were finally coming true. She wasn't going to be alone anymore. She was going to belong again.

Part of a family just like everyone else.

"Let me feel."

She'd barely registered the words before Joe's larger, warmer hand was pushing hers aside and flattening against her stomach—covering far more of her than she had.

She wanted to tell him she was sure it was too soon for him to feel anything on the outside. Should have told him.

But she couldn't make herself end the contact. His hand felt so good on her. So right.

She was so in trouble.

UP BEFORE ELISE the next morning, Sunday, Joe pulled on basketball shorts, a shirt and shoes, skipping his shower and shave altogether. One didn't need to smell or look good to sweat like a pig on a basketball court. He grabbed some cold pizza from the doggie bag he'd brought home from dinner the night before and, slice in hand, practically ran out the side door to his car.

After the night he'd just spent, he needed to exhaust his libido before interacting with his business partner again. And rid himself of some testosterone, too. He was losing perspective, thinking she needed his protection.

Thinking he had some sort of ownership of her.

A business commodity, indeed. An investment.

A sexy woman.

He should be shot.

"I CAN'T THANK YOU ENOUGH—"

"Hold it." Elise forestalled anything else Adam Fallow might say. "Like I said on the phone last night, this is breakfast. Nothing more." Thank goodness morning sickness had passed and she could actually eat the morning meal.

Adam pulled on the heavy glass door leading into the posh bakery-café in Grand Rapids, held it for her. "You're giving my request honest consideration," he told her. "I'm grateful for that."

She didn't want him grateful. She wanted a sign that she could walk away free and clear.

They walked past the bakery area through an atrium filled with plants and were shown to their booth, given menus and offered coffee. Almost immediately a smiling young waitress approached. And then Elise was alone with a tall, good-looking, sandy-haired man who, even in cotton shorts and a pullover, inspired confidence. His smile was kind.

"I need to make certain that you understand that I'm not leaning toward granting your request," she told him, looking him directly in the eye.

His nod was slow. "I do."

"I'm also not one to be swayed by emotion. And I can see through manipulation before it even gets started."

"I figured that out months ago." His reply was dry, but the smile on his face softened the response. "It's not like I've done any of this before, but I asked around enough to know that the way you did things was most definitely not the norm."

"I like to be prepared."

"Some things can't be predicted or planned for."

He hit the one hard fact she couldn't get around—ever. The one thing in life that still scared her to death.

Her juice arrived along with his coffee.

"What do you do for a living?"

"I'm an engineer by day," he said, naming a technology company with a local branch. "But that sounds more grandiose at the moment than it is. I stayed in college for my doctorate and so I'm relatively new to the workforce. I am currently, therefore, little more than an assistant who's good at drawing..."

She sipped her juice. Ordered an omelet when their waitress returned, paid attention while he asked for scrambled eggs with sausage, whole wheat toast and fruit. He treated the waitress politely, with respect. And he made intelligent nutrition choices without being obsessive about it.

"Why did you answer my donor ad?"

He didn't even blink at her bluntness. "I'm an engineer during the day, but an inventor at night. I've designed a new gearshift that has received some real interest from a manufacturer and I needed money quickly to get the patent process started on it before I felt comfortable with the risk of shipping it out for testing. Marie and I had life insurance on me, but none on her. I'd used up most of our savings on her funeral expenses."

A commendable account. Still, there were other ways to get money.

"What about a small-business loan?" She'd taken out a few.

"I'm in debt with student loans already. I'd always said I'd only pursue the inventing if I could do it without going further into debt. There's no guarantee in that business, not even a fifty-percent chance that I'll sell something and actually make money at it—which means less than a fifty-percent chance that I'd be able to pay back the loan with the earnings of the business."

And still he tried.

She could relate to that.

People came and went around them, families filled the tables opposite and behind theirs, many of them dressed in church clothes.

Imagining scenes like this was why Elise had always shied away from eating out alone. Scenes like this were the substance of her dreams.

And his?

"What do you think Marie would have thought of your decision?"

"She'd have hated it if she were still alive."

"But since she's not, you didn't care?"

The question was far too familiar for two strangers who'd just met. And yet the reason for their meeting, the fact that she might be carrying his seed in her body, the thing he was asking of her, gave license where she would never otherwise have taken it.

"I cared." That's all he said.

"And?"

Adam hesitated, spun his coffee mug around with his thumb on the handle.

And then he looked over at her. "I'm not sure how to answer that."

"Honestly might be good."

"Honestly might be construed as emotional manipulation."

Touché.

"I'll take that chance."

"Marie's death showed me too late the irreplaceable value of something I took largely for granted. Having loved ones to come home to at night." He was looking down and paused for a long moment.

Elise wanted to tell him stop. She'd heard enough. But her throat was so dry she couldn't speak.

He glanced up, watching her as he finished. "I thought she'd support my decision to give someone else the chance to gain a loved one."

There were tears in Elise's eyes as she sat back to allow the waitress to set down her food.

JOE FOUND ELISE out on the screened patio, rocking in the dusk on a white wicker love-seat swing Sunday evening.

"You okay?"

"Yeah."

That made one of them. He couldn't get her out of his mind. Couldn't find his equilibrium.

Couldn't stay away from her.

"You sure? Nothing's hurting? You aren't sick?"

"I'm fine, Joe, really."

He thought she glanced at him—her head turned in his direction—but he couldn't see her expression.

"You weren't here when I got back from the gym." And that fact hadn't been far from his mind most of the day.

"I met Adam Fallow for breakfast."

Panic shot through him. And then was gone. Joe sat in the adjacent wicker chair, trying to find a logical explanation for the emotions he kept experiencing. And failing.

"And?"

"He's a nice guy. Better than nice."

So the two of them could forge a bond through their children, fall in love—she was already obviously in like—and eventually marry and share the family they both wanted.

Even without the love they could marry. Unions happened for all kinds of reasons, many less compelling than a shared desire for children.

Leaning forward with his elbows on his knees, he studied what he could see of the legs of the chair beneath him.

"Have you made a decision?"

She didn't answer immediately.

"No."

Her answer was a relief. Tension that had been building all day dissipated enough to show him how tightly he was wrung.

"You want to talk about it?"

She rocked some more, her enlarged belly made more obvious by the way she was cupping it with her hands. Joe tried not to stare. And couldn't stop the flow of blood to his groin as he remembered the way that mound had felt under his hand the night before.

He was sick. A pervert. And never knew the tendency could be so latent. Why hadn't he seen signs before now?

And what in the hell did he do about it?

"I don't want to talk about anything," she said slowly. "I've always handled things on my own. I'm comfortable with that."

Fair enough. He wouldn't push her. Never had.

He'd never had this gripping need to be given access to her intimate confidences before, either.

He should go in, watch a movie. Tomorrow began another week and he was tired.

An evening breeze blew up off the river, sliding gently through the screened walls of the porch. If this were his house, he'd sleep out here. The daybed along the far wall looked comfortable enough.

Maybe someday, when Elise was out, he'd give it a try.

"The problem is—" her voice softly broke the stillness "—I'm driving myself crazy with circular thoughts. I just keep going around and around and can't seem to sort things out."

So did she want to chat with him or not?

"Did you call your doctor friend?"

"No."

"Why not?"

"Because my sex life is not something I'd ever discuss with Thomas."

Whoa. Joe was glad no lights were on in the screened porch. The shadows safely concealed his expression.

"I understand," he said, when he didn't at all.

Had she done something other than *talk* with this Fallow guy? Or was she contemplating doing so? Had they already discussed the possibility of marriage and she was considering the ramifications of that? Wondering if she could sleep with him?

Or was she just turned on by the guy and worried that desire would influence her ability to make a healthy and fair decision?

Was there such a thing as fair when you considered equally compelling but opposing needs?

Was it fair that she was sitting over there, not three feet away, barefoot and beautiful, wearing little more than a light, cotton, sleeveless shift over the stomach he'd touched for the first time the day before, completely off-limits and talking to him about her sexuality?

"You do?" Her voice was low, falling between them as tangibly as a touch.

"No."

"What don't you understand?"

"What your sexuality has to do with whether or not you release fertility records."

Okay, maybe he got that part, but he could be

wrong. He hoped he was wrong. And that was what he really didn't understand.

Why did it matter to him if she slept with this other guy? They'd been sleeping with other people for fifteen years and it had never caused even a ripple in the waters of his life.

"It has nothing to do with it."

Joe's mind quieted. Stopped working altogether for a moment while he changed course, adjusted his thinking.

"Now I'm really confused."

The large sigh she took was not comforting. "My…sexuality doesn't have anything to do with whether or not I agree to unseal the records. But it's part of the muck I can't seem to wade through to get to any clear position."

"What can I do to help?"

"Talk to me."

But she'd already said she didn't need to discuss anything.

"You want to talk to me about sex?" he asked hesitantly.

"I think I have to."

Joe had a feeling he should have turned in when he'd had the chance.

CHAPTER TWELVE

"Would you like to go inside?"

Elise shook her head at Joe's question and then realized he probably couldn't see her. "I'd rather be out here."

He had sounded so calm, so businesslike. Which was precisely what she should have been. And why she had to continue.

"This is really difficult for me," she told him.

"If you'd rather not—"

"Joe, I'm screwing up. Big time. I'm driving myself crazy. I can't think straight. And the one thing I know is that I have to do whatever is necessary to preserve you and me—our partnership, our working relationship. B&R."

When he moved, she thought he was going to walk out on her. And wondered if that would have been best when he sat down beside her on the swing instead.

"There's nothing wrong here," he said, leaning over to look her in the eye. "I'm here because I want to be. I told you that. You've been through hell with me, Elise. You know that. And now, for the first time, you need me. I'm happy to return the favor. I mean it."

Oh, boy, did she need him. He had no idea.

"You're making this so hard."

He sat back. "Tell me what—"

"Just listen," she interrupted quickly. "Let me say what I have to say before I lose my courage and then tell me what you think."

He nodded. He wasn't smiling.

"I could be committing suicide here," she blurted. "I would never in a million years consider doing this if so much weren't at stake. But then, I'd never in a million years have believed I could ever be in this position."

"Having four babies instead of one, you mean?"

Elise almost told him to forget it. She was making a terrible mistake. Humiliating herself for nothing. And then Joe moved, his shoulder touching hers, and she was in a nervous tizzy all over again.

"No, Joe, that's not what I mean." She took a deep breath, gave herself one last chance to change her mind. "My mind is consumed with this to the point that I can no longer think straight," she said, as much for her own benefit as his. "And the only thing that occurs to me is to be completely honest with you. That way we can deal with the situation and move on."

Or, rather, back. Somehow she had to find normal

again. At least with Joe. All the stability she'd built since growing up was based on Joe and B&R.

"So talk, and we'll handle it."

From his mouth to God's ears. Let it be that easy.

"I want it clear that I want nothing from you here." She couldn't continue if that wasn't understood. "I'm not looking, or hoping, for any action on your part."

"Okay."

His shoulder was still touching hers. It was a test.

"Remember when we did that team-building seminar last fall?"

"With Glynnis Elrod."

"Yeah. She talked about the dead elephant in the middle of the table and how, if left there unattended, it would really start to stink, but if acknowledged and dealt with, it could be removed."

"Right. You either ignore your company's issues and they escalate and eventually hurt and sometimes cripple the company, or you admit they exist, talk about them, find solutions and move on."

He'd paid attention. She wasn't surprised.

"Well, I've got a dead elephant on our table."

"This is about B&R?"

"Everything to do with me and you is about B&R."

And if she didn't quit stalling, she was going to suffocate on her tension. Or start to like the smell of dead elephant.

"The thing is, Joe…" She leaned to her side, resting her elbow on the arm of the swing. Breaking all physical contact with him.

"Yes?"

"I met with Adam Fallow this morning. He's attractive, intelligent, ethical. He's a gentleman and he made me laugh."

"You said this didn't have anything to do with the fertility decision."

"I went in hopes of getting some clarity about what I should do. I brought him out, gave him hope and wasted an entire morning for both of us because I can't think clearly about anything. I sat across from him and thought about your shoulders and how they were all I could think about at dinner Saturday night. He smiled and I, God help me, thought about what happened outside the bathroom door Friday morning. He glanced at my stomach— at possibly his babies growing there—and I relived the warmth of your hand, touching me."

He didn't respond. Didn't move at all.

"He's a nice man, more than nice. I really like him. I want to help him. And you're getting in the way, Joe." This wasn't going to work if she was going to call the elephant a horse. "Well, you aren't, but my thoughts of you are."

Or a cow.

"Not my thoughts of you," she amended. "Okay, the truth is, for some inexplicable reason, I'm suddenly finding you irresistible. Sexually.

As in everything you do turns me on and I can't stand it. I'm losing my mind. I don't want to have sex with you! Not that you're asking, I understand that. Not that you're the least bit interested. But even if you were, I don't want that. You're the best friend I've ever had. I like it that way. I need it that way. You're my business partner, my career."

She came to a halt only because she couldn't think of anything else to add that wouldn't just be repeating herself. The resulting silence was more humiliating, more painful than speaking had been.

At last she said, "I'm scared to death of ruining everything by having inappropriate feelings I can't seem to help."

He still hadn't moved. Not even a finger. If he'd blinked, she hadn't seen it.

"Like I said, I'm not asking you for anything," she reiterated when she could stand the silence no longer. Had she already blown their relationship by bringing this up? Surely she and Joe as a team were strong enough to get beyond it. They'd faced some pretty steep challenges over the years and always surmounted them—together. Where one of them failed, the other succeeded. Where one had weakness the other had strength.

"This isn't an invitation, or a come on or some kind of plea for you to take pity on me and put me out of my misery."

She'd die first.

But what a death it would be. The foreign being that had possessed her body recently wouldn't be quiet, even now. She'd known she was in serious trouble that morning when Adam had mentioned his sperm and she'd thought of a part of Joe's body she'd had no business visiting, ever. Not even in her mind.

Had Joe fallen asleep?

More likely, he was angry. And she didn't blame him. Dead elephants usually weren't pleasant. Removing them wasn't pleasant. But the end result made it worth the effort.

Even now, sitting here completely mortified and hating herself, she could feel the teasing of butterflies in her private places.

"Say something."

"I don't know what to say."

He didn't sound angry. Was that pain in his voice? Or pity?

"Curse at me," she offered. "Tell me I'm imagining it all. That you've never given me any reason to feel these things. Tell me you're moving out. Just tell me something."

"I don't know what to say," he repeated.

What good did it do to acknowledge a dead elephant if they were just going to leave it lying in the middle of the table?

"The truth would be good," she finally said, cold and then hot and then cold again. "I'm being painfully honest here, Joe, in the hopes that we can handle the situation and then forget about it. We can't leave it just hanging here between us. Not with both of us knowing about it."

He turned, reached for the standing lamp beside him, clicked it on. "I need light."

"Okay." Elise blinked, squinting against the brightness, and forced herself to look at him. It was one of the hardest things she'd ever done, putting her face out there for him to see. She wondered if how small she felt showed.

"You want honesty, I'll give it to you," he finally said, the words more biting than kind. Yet his eyes weren't glacial, as she'd seen them be when Joe was really angry about something. Like the time they'd seen a woman haul a two-year-old kid out of a restaurant by the arm for spilling his milk and slapping him repeatedly on the sidewalk just outside the door.

He'd reported the woman to child protective services.

His gaze was devouring every inch of Elise's face. Her neck and throat. Then back to her eyes. The cords in his neck were so tight she could see them move with every breath he took.

Elise swallowed, scared to death. What had she done?

If only she could take it all back. Apologize. Wipe away the words she'd put in his mind, words that might have just killed a solid, fifteen-year relationship.

Elise wanted to run inside, to throw herself on

her bed and cry until there were no more tears, but she was rooted to the white wicker swing beside him until she knew he was done with her.

"The truth is you aren't alone."

Of course she wasn't, he was sitting right there. What did that have to do with…

Sweat soaked the back of her dress. "What do you mean?"

"Only for me it started two weeks ago at the clinic when I saw the skin on your stomach and wondered if it was as soft and satiny as it looked."

She must not be hearing right. Or she'd taken leave of her senses. Elise tried to focus. To understand. She couldn't pull her gaze away from him.

"There are some small scars on my sides, but you can't tell unless you feel the skin there," she said inanely. "It's not completely smooth at the seams."

"I wanted to kiss your belly button."

Her crotch was on fire. This couldn't be happening.

They couldn't let it happen.

"What's the matter with us?" she asked, at a total loss for one of the first times she could ever remember. "It would never work. We run a business together. We can't afford the conflict of interest. I'm having four babies. You shudder at the thought of even one. We've been together for fifteen years and you've never turned me on before."

"You have such a way with words." Joe chuckled

softly, deep in his throat, and Elise wanted to throw herself in his arms, get lost there in forgetfulness.

"Well," she challenged instead, "have I ever turned you on before?"

"No."

Not even a little bit? She was ashamed of the question that popped instantly to mind. She deserved better than that. And so did he.

"I think what we have here that's different from before," he continued, his voice strained, but lighter, "is proximity. We're two adults, a man and woman, living in close quarters and sharing a somewhat intimate situation—the birthing of your children. And for you, I suspect some of it's hormonal. As soon as we get through this and I move back home, the feelings will disappear as though they never existed."

The hope his words elicited made her light-headed. "Do you really think so?"

"We know each other too well for it to be anything else. If we were going to have the hots for each other, they'd have hit long before now."

He sounded so sure. And he made sense.

"I'll have the babies, go back to work, and you'll just be the guy who stops by my office to give me problems to solve."

"And to give you new clients to support you."

"We just have to get through the next few months—which really shouldn't be all that hard considering that I'm going to be as big as a house pretty soon and having sex won't be an option."

"This will all be over soon," he said, almost as though the words were some kind of mantra.

He thought her stomach was sexy. The idea pleased her far too much, but that would pass, too.

"So we're agreed that what we feel is circumstantial, we've acknowledged it, decided to take no action, understanding that it will dissipate on its own at the end of this current project."

"Correct."

She could live with that.

"WHAT ARE YOU GOING TO DO about Fallow?" Joe asked Monday night over the taco salad dinner she'd prepared. He'd had a frustrating day, putting out fires rather than making deals. And he was going on too little sleep, having spent the night fighting the knowledge that Elise wanted him. Fighting off mental images of her naked beneath him. On top of him. In the shower with him.

And fighting his body's response to the images.

"Nothing, for now."

That wasn't clear enough to satisfy his crankiness. "You're telling him no."

She should. Get the guy out of her life. They didn't need any further complications.

Besides, Elise was vulnerable right now, hormonally horny. And perfectly safe with him. He couldn't say the same for any other guy.

"I'm telling him that I'm not prepared to make a decision one way or the other. There's no rush.

It's not like he's ready to have children in the next month or two. Probably not even the next year or two. And if it turns out that Danny and Ellen and Grace and Thomas are his, it wouldn't make a difference right now even if I ever *did* agree to allow him some rights."

Joe had been spoiling for a fight. Now his mood was just plain sour. He thought the guy should be gone for good. Now. "He might want to be involved with their gestation, with the delivery. He might want to get to know you better."

He should be shot for egging her on. For making any of this more difficult for her than it already was.

"I'm not responsible for his fate," she said. "What I do about the future is going to have to wait until the future gets here and I can figure it all out."

"Would you like me to meet him?"

She set down her fork, wiped her mouth. "Why would I?" She hadn't met his eyes since they'd parted company on the porch the night before.

"I'm a pretty good judge of people."

"I already know he's a good guy, Joe. That doesn't mean I want to share my family with him."

Joe wasn't all that hungry. "I think you should let me call my dad. Just in case. He might have some advice, something gleaned from thirty more years' experience with living than either of us have."

"Do your parents know I'm pregnant?"

"Not yet."

"If it weren't for asking your father's advice, were you planning to tell them?"

He honestly hadn't thought about it. "You're my business partner," he said now. "It would have come out eventually."

Like the next Christmas dinner his parents invited her to share. She'd been there every Christmas he'd been married to Kelly.

"They're live-and-let-live kind of people, Elise. You know that. They aren't going to judge what you're doing. My sisters and mother are going to be thrilled at the idea of four new babies in a room at once. No need to fight over who gets to hold and who has to watch."

Elise's frown softened and he was struck by how sensitive she really was, how well she'd hidden that part of herself all these years. And how dense he'd been not to figure it out anyway.

He was struck with a powerful urge to kiss her one more time.

He didn't act on it.

"Would you mind if I was there when you spoke to your father?" Her question, her relatively easy acquiescence, took him by surprise.

"We could have them over here for dinner, if you'd like," he offered. She was a homebody, too. Seemed more comfortable in her own space.

"I'd rather meet them out someplace neutral."

Still amazed that this beautiful, self-possessed, sometimes bossy woman had admitted that she was turned on by him, Joe agreed to arrange something for later that week.

And was glad that his parents weren't going to descend upon them here in the secret world he and Elise were sharing.

JOE'S SMELL WAS EVERYWHERE. Standing in the shower Tuesday morning, soaping herself, Elise closed her eyes, sniffed his aftershave and could almost imagine that it was Joe's hand sliding across her stomach, her breasts. Joe's fingers brushing her nipples.

They hardened instantly and she dropped the soap as her eyes flew open. What in hell was she doing?

Speaking silently to the children she'd not yet birthed, telling them about the home they were coming to, the life she hoped to give them, Elise finished her shower, sped through the kitchen to grab a banana and granola bar on her way out the door, and made it to work in record time.

It was only as she sat at her desk half an hour later that she remembered she forgot to fill Samantha and Darin's dry-food bowl. They were going to be pissed as hell at her by the time she got home that night.

She didn't blame them. She was pissed at herself, too.

"OF COURSE YOU HAVE no legal concern whatso-ever." Joe's dad, shorter and broader and grayer than his son, looked exactly like Joe when he smiled. His eyes softened as Joe's did, showing heart behind the testosterone. The man set his reading glasses on the table beside his ginger ale, handing her back the documentation Joe had sent to him earlier that day. "But that's not what you're asking, is it?"

Sitting at the white-linen-covered table at the elder Mr. Bennett's favorite steak house on Thursday after work, waiting for dinner to be delivered, Elise shook her head. She'd dressed carefully for the meeting Joe had told her about the night before, choosing a pink tweed suit fitted with a stretch panel.

Joe's parents had greeted her with hugs and kisses, delighted she'd had Joe share her news with them.

"It's a tough situation," Edward Bennett said, with a glance at his wife. "And maybe more up Clara's alley."

"What would *you* do?" Joe asked the plump, gray-haired woman sitting on the other side of him. He'd barely touched his beer.

"I don't know, son." The two exchanged a glance that was filled with affection—and something more. A sense of knowing each other deeply, maybe respecting each other. Clara reached for her purse, and Joe grabbed it from beneath her chair, handing it to her.

Elise wasn't surprised at his attentiveness, but

rather surprised that she'd never paid attention before to how helpful her partner was with everyone. Of course Joe was charming, she knew that, but she'd taken for granted the tiny things he did all the time to make life easier for everyone around him.

Of course, she'd taken his good looks for granted, too.

Clara pulled out a picture, handed it to Elise. She'd seen it before. A larger version of it was on the mantel in Joe's parents' house.

"Those seven kids are my life," she told her. "Every memory I have, of any of them, is gold in my pocket. They are a part of me. But not because of biological science. They're a part of me because I fed them and bathed them. I dried their tears and heard their first words. I laughed and played with them."

She was describing Elise's lifelong dream.

"And so did Edward," Clara said, as though the words held specific significance. "A seed doesn't make a father. And neither does marriage or proximity. The only thing that makes a father is the willingness to share a child's experience of growing up. To teach and watch, to protect and provide—and also to allow. Parents must be willing to stand back and watch as their children find themselves, so that each child becomes the unique individual he or she was meant to be."

Joe, unsmiling, was staring at his beer. And Elise

recalled many of the stories he'd told of his years growing up in a too-small house with too many children. He'd never been able to sit and watch an entire program on television uninterrupted. What Clara called allowance, Joe had seen as chaos.

"I don't believe that a parent," Clara went on, "if he's only with a child part-time, can know that child well enough to know when to stand back. I also don't believe a child—any child—should suffer in order to make parents happy."

Tears in her eyes, feeling some release inside, Elise nodded. "Adam Fallow is a good man with a heartbreaking story, but my job is to protect my children, to make certain that whatever decision I make is one that will make them happier—not anyone else."

"That's what I think," Joe's mom said. "But I'm just a housewife who worked part-time for the phone company to help make ends meet until Ed's practice was firmly established."

"Don't kid yourself," Ed chimed in. "Clara's the smartest woman I've ever met."

Joe's continued silence bothered Elise. Was he seeing himself in his mother's description? Joe Bennett, the man proximity couldn't make into a father because the desire just wasn't there? And if he was, didn't he know that that was perfectly all right? He was a great human being, a loyal and true and dedicated friend, an honest businessman, a generous employer and an attentive son.

No wonder she'd stuck with him for more than fifteen years.

Or maybe he was just bored with the conversation…

CHAPTER THIRTEEN

THEIR STEAKS ARRIVED. Famished all of a sudden, Elise had a feeling she was going to eat every bite.

Clara wanted to know when the babies were due, what she was going to name them and whether she was going to hire someone to come in during the day or send them to day care.

"Joe's oldest sister, Kate, is sending her youngest off to college this month," Clara said, her eyes getting a familiar glint—one Elise had seen in Joe's eyes often enough to know that it meant something was cooking. "She's been a stay-at-home mom since she married at eighteen. Watching four babies all day would be the perfect antidote to empty-nest syndrome."

"Kate's only forty-one," Joe said. "Maybe she wants some freedom for the first time in her life. She could go to college, have a career—"

"Joseph," Clara interrupted, patting his hand, the only adornment on her fingers the wide gold band Edward had put there more than forty years earlier. "For such a smart man you do tend to miss the boat at times."

"What do you mean?" Joe's tone reflected his confusion. "You don't think Kate's looking forward to doing whatever she wants to do?"

"What your mother is trying to say is that all your oldest sister has ever wanted to do is be a mother." Ed sawed off another piece of bacon-wrapped filet mignon. "From the time she was old enough to walk, the only toys she was interested in were dolls and bottles. Don't you remember, when the last four of your brothers and sisters arrived, she couldn't wait to get home from school to help take care of *her* babies? Your mom and I are extremely concerned that she's going to sink into serious depression when Kyle leaves."

Fork suspended over his loaded baked potato, Joe said, "Kate? You've got to be kidding! She's always been the most cheerful one of us."

"She's always been doing what her heart most desired—she's felt fulfilled."

"Do you really think she'd be interested in helping me?" Elise couldn't hold back any longer. For the first time since the initial ultrasound had revealed four fetuses, she felt like she'd actually be able to pull this whole quadruplet thing off. Like things were going to fall into place somehow, that they'd be okay.

"I know she would," Clara said, her face alight with pleasure, as though she was being relieved of a great worry. "But I don't want you to think you *have* to consider her if you have other plans," she added.

Elise teared up again. "Sorry," she said, embarrassed while she waited for the emotion to pass. "I've never been a person who cries easily. But you have no idea how much this would mean to me. I've been in a panic trying to figure out what I'm going to do, how I can leave my babies with a stranger. Obviously she'd need help, too, at least until they're old enough to hold their own bottles, but I'd trust my babies to Kate in a heartbeat."

Not only did Elise know the woman, she'd seen Kate's knack for mothering in action—she'd had three kids in diapers at the same time. The woman was gentle, firm and had the patience of a saint. And she was Joe's sister. Safe. Solid. Almost family.

She reminded Elise of her own mother.

Clara dug her cell phone out of her purse. Joe took it from her.

"You eat, Mom. You know how you hate cold steak. I'll call Kate."

"To HEAR MOM TELL IT, you'd think we were all one big happy family when I was growing up," Joe said, frowning as he turned the Lexus toward Lowell.

"You don't think your parents were happy?"

He didn't know what he thought anymore. "I guess I always assumed they weren't. Their stuff was broken by one kid or another on a regular basis. They were always trying to drive one of us somewhere. They had to deal with homework, endless carpooling, mending, bathing, bandaging—and all of that after dinner when they were tired. We kids all whined about everything from meals to bedtime a whole lot more than we were grateful for anything. We fought, too. There was never any peace."

He wanted peace. For as long as he could remember, that was all he'd ever wanted. How many times had he climbed the stairs to the attic as a boy, escaping to a place away from everyone else?

"Kate took the brunt of helping out with the younger kids—then married straight out of high school. I thought she'd be ecstatic just to leave home and finally having some freedom and peace. But within four years she had three kids of her own."

"What about Kenny?" Elise asked. "He's second oldest, right? Does he feel like you do?"

"I doubt it," Joe said. "Kenny was the space cadet. Everything rolled off his back—still does. If there was a fight, he could be sitting right in the middle of it and not even know it was going on."

"Sounds like my brother, Danny. We girls would be carrying on, laughing, fighting, Baby Grace would be crying, and he'd sit there watching cartoons and not even seem to hear us."

It was hard for him to picture Elise in such a setting. The woman he knew had always been alone.

He decided to take the scenic route and turned along the river, slowing for the hills and bends. Tall trees on either side of the road blocked out the moon.

"I've heard lots of stories that involved you helping the younger kids with one thing or another—like the time you stayed up half the night in your bedroom helping Bradley with a project for school," Elise said. "Did you really hate it that much?"

Joe didn't want to go back to those days. He'd rather concentrate on the woman sitting next to him. The woman who'd seen his potential, shared his vision and stood by his side making it possible for him to live the life he wanted to live.

"I did what had to be done," he answered her eventually. "Bradley's school project was kind of fun, as I recall. Playing Chutes and Ladders a million times when I'd rather have been on the basketball court with my friends was not."

It wasn't a matter of the various chores. He'd always hated taking out the trash—still hated it. But he made trash, so he took it out. Life required chores—Joe had no problem with that. It was the constant, endless needs and wants of others that made him cringe.

"It was never enough."

"What wasn't?"

"No matter how much Mom or Dad or Kate or I did, there was always someone who needed something, who wasn't happy with something. When it comes to kids, no matter how much you do, it's never enough."

Joe heard the words and wished he'd bitten his tongue. This was Elise, the woman he'd always been able to spout off to, the one person he could tell anything to and know that she'd neither judge nor humor him. But now she was also a woman who was pregnant with four kids.

"I think the key to that lies in what your mother said, at least partially," Elise said. Her tone wasn't defensive. Apparently they were still talking, airing their views, just as they always had. "There comes a time when your contribution to a project, whatever it is, is to stand back and allow it to take its own course."

Maybe because he was out of his element, living outside his own space, his own routine, outside the life he'd carefully created for himself, her words made some kind of sense to him.

"Happiness is largely an illusion, isn't it?" she asked, her face turned away as she stared out her side window. "It's always that elusive something just out of our reach, yet we spend our lives constantly reaching anyway. Unless, like your parents, we simply decide to be happy where we are and find that joy and peace and contentment had been in our grasp all along."

He didn't think he agreed with her. But couldn't find a logical argument to refute what she'd said.

"Are you happy, Joe?"

"Absolutely." Some of the time. Of course he was.

"Happier alone than when you were living with Kelly?"

"Overall." Life was entirely peaceful. A little

boring sometimes, maybe, but he had the canoe and sports and friends and business meetings.

"Well, *I* wasn't," she told him. "I love my job. I love my house. I was happy at work, but I hated coming home alone every night. I hated crashing your family parties, or being alone on holidays. I hated not having people to care for or share good news with. I hated not belonging to anyone."

Joe supposed he'd hate that, too.

"Having you around this past month," she went on, "has been really different, and a little hard to adjust to. But at the same time it's given me a taste of how great it's going to be to have other people around sharing the everyday things we do by rote and take so much for granted."

It was nice hearing the shower running when you weren't in it, Joe thought.

"I'm sure you're just pulling at the bit, dying to get back home alone, aren't you?"

"Maybe a little," he said. And maybe not much at all. But he wasn't even going to start thinking along those lines.

ELISE HAD THE LAST of her every-third-week doctor's appointments the next day. From this point on she'd be going every two weeks until closer to term when, if she was still at home, the visits would become once a week.

Joe opted to remain in the waiting room while Elise was examined—not wanting to tempt his libido again with that much intimacy—but he was inordinately glad he'd insisted on being included in the visits when they all sat in her doctor's office following the exam.

"You're still okay for all normal activity, within reason," Dr. Braden told her patient. "No heavy lifting or mountain climbing. But judging by how quickly your measurements are changing, I'm guessing it'll only be another month at the most before you'll need to take your leave from work."

Her leave from work? It sounded as though the doctor and Elise had already discussed the plan.

"Why will she need to leave work so soon? Is something wrong?"

"No. So far she's textbook for a perfect quad pregnancy." Dr. Braden shook her head, never losing her serious demeanor. "But the babies are going to start growing more now and things are going to get pretty crowded in there fairly quickly. We expect premature delivery in multiple pregnancies, but the closer we can get Elise to thirty-four or thirty-six weeks gestation, the better the chances of delivering four well babies. In order to do that, she'll need to spend a good bit of time lying down. As a matter of fact—" the woman put her reading glasses on top of Elise's file on a desk so strewn with papers Joe thought it was a wonder she could find anything "—I'm expecting to have to prescribe *full* bed rest before we get through here. My hope is to be able to keep Elise at home, but it's not uncommon for a mother of multiples to spend the last weeks of her pregnancy in the hospital."

Joe's heart began to race. Why hadn't Elise told him this pregnancy of hers was so dangerous? The more the doctor talked, the more he realized how easily he could lose her in the course of the next months.

And the more determined he grew to make certain he did everything in his power to ensure that didn't happen. Whatever it took.

"I want you to go down to the lab sometime in the next few days," Dr. Braden continued with what seemed to be never-ending instruction. "I'd like another diabetes test just to be safe. Your blood pressure's normal and the swelling in your hands and feet is normal, and that's all good news. I just want to make certain we stay on top of things so we don't have any scares down the road."

Elise nodded. And then the doctor smiled. Looked at Joe.

"We heard five healthy heartbeats this morning."

He almost choked. "Five?"

"Mommy's and four babies."

Oh. Well, that was okay, then. The four-member crew they were in the process of bringing aboard were keeping up to speed.

Elise talked about the heartbeats all the way out to their cars.

Joe kind of wished he'd heard them, too.

"I CALLED KATE BACK today," Joe said that evening as they sat down to a dinner of pasta broccoli casserole and wheat bread from the bakery on the first floor of their office building.

Elise looked up, her appetite immediately stunted. "Did she change her mind about wanting the job?"

"On the contrary." He chewed as though nothing was wrong. But then, Joe had always been able to take things in stride better than she could. Once he got his mind wrapped around something, that was. "She's onboard to start as soon as you get put on bed rest. She'll come before I leave for work in the morning and stay until I get home."

Elise stared at him. "You told her you're staying with me?" Not that she minded. He'd been the one who'd been adamant about not telling anyone. And she understood why. He didn't want anyone getting any ideas.

Joe was not and was never going to be a family man. Since his divorce, he'd been very careful not to give his family any idea or hope that he'd ever hook up with someone again.

Since their staff had found out about their living arrangement, he'd gone out of his way not to have a private moment with her that could be misconstrued.

"Kate's always been good for a secret," Joe said now. "And after hearing what the doctor said today, I knew we were going to need help."

We. The pronoun sounded so good Elise

couldn't help smiling. As for the rest, she was still set on being the first known mother of quads in Michigan not to be confined to bed before the birth.

AFTER DINNER, JOE ASKED HER if she wanted to take a walk.

"Dr. Braden said you should get as much moderate exercise as you can while you can," he told her. And he needed a break from being alone with her in the quiet intimacy of her home.

The entire weekend stretched out before them. They could get naked and stay that way for two full days without arousing any suspicions anywhere.

Damn. What was he thinking?

"Let me get my running shoes."

She'd be covering up those bare feet. That was progress. Now if only he could find a way to talk her into wearing a blanket that covered every inch of her, in place of the spaghetti-strapped flowery dress she had on.

"Did you call that Fallow guy today?" he asked as they strolled along Main Street.

"Yes. I told him I'd let him know in a week, and today was it."

Being outside wasn't helping Joe's tension all that much. "What'd you tell him?"

"That I wasn't going to make a decision until after the babies were born."

It was better than nothing, though Joe would've

preferred a solid no. He didn't like the guy looming out there.

And was really uncomfortable with the realization that he had no logical reason for feeling that way.

Elise with other men had never bothered him before. And he had absolutely no ownership over these babies she was birthing. No *interest* in ownership.

"I told him that if something changed and he had reason to need an answer sooner to call me."

"He has your phone number?"

"I gave it to him today."

Joe's mood didn't improve, but he managed to keep his mouth shut against the negative admonition he had the urge to put forth.

A woman with three kids was coming the other way. She had two by the hand and the third, a boy who looked to be about seven, was walking off to the side, dragging a stick in the gutter. The woman's shoulders sagged—probably so she could reach the little hands at her sides. Her makeup, if she'd had any on, had long since worn off. And the child on her right was crying.

A far cry from the peace and relaxation he and Elise were sharing.

Unfortunately, he could relate to the woman. And to the son with the stick in the gutter, creating his own world to escape the one in which he lived. Wrapping himself in make-believe, in plans for how he'd change his life when he was old enough.

Because when you had younger siblings, there was always more that had to be done. As soon as you got one settled, another needed something.

He couldn't face the thought of living his adult life feeling that way—as though no matter what he did, when he went to bed at night he'd have to feel guilty for the things he was leaving undone, the people he was letting down. As though no matter what he'd done, it was never enough.

They passed the now silent Lowell showboat docked in its permanent home beside the Flat River Grill. The town hosted concerts on the decked-out paddlewheel vessel every Thursday all summer, but he hadn't been to one in years.

"When I was a kid there used to be vaudeville-type shows on that thing every night," he said, stopping to lean on the rail of the sidewalk bridge over the river.

"All summer long?" She'd stopped beside him, her arms only inches from his on the rail.

"Probably not," he said, thinking back. "But it seemed that way. I'm guessing there was a season—two weeks, a month, I don't know."

"Was it run by the town then?"

"I don't know that, either, but they had some fairly big-name entertainers. And there were these 'end men'—they'd probably be outlawed today, but they were local entertainers who blackened their faces and doubled as ushers and gave comedic relief throughout the performance.

"The boat used to come up the river every

evening before the show with all the colorful lights on its deck glowing and music playing."

He'd watched the boat from a corner close to Elise's house every night he could get there. Those had been magical moments.

"Did you ever go to one of the shows?"

"Yes." He smiled. "Each summer Mom and Dad bought three tickets to seven shows. We'd each get a date night, just one of us kids and the two of them."

She turned, and he was hard pressed to keep his grin, her lips were so close. "They went seven times?"

"Yeah. I never thought about it at the time," he admitted, glancing back at the boat as he wondered how many other things about his childhood he'd framed incorrectly. "I just saw it as a duty they did to give us each the experience, but in reality, they were entertaining themselves sevenfold."

"Pretty smart, if you ask me."

And kind of romantic, he thought, if you didn't consider that each of their dates included a kid.

"I've always been meaning to come down for one of the concerts, but never seem to get around to it," she said.

"Next year, we'll go four times and take one baby each time." Joe was joking, of course.

"Yeah, right!" Elise laughed, moving on.

And he was kind of disappointed.

THEY WALKED AGAIN on Saturday. This time Elise took Joe to the cemetery. The local florist had been keeping flowers in the urn, the grass was lush green and freshly cut. There wasn't a weed to be found.

She felt uncertain.

"I…um…Joe, meet my mom and dad and Danny, Ellen and Baby Grace," she said, pointing out the headstones.

He moved slowly and silently down the row, reading each one.

"Do you do the flowers?" he asked.

"No. I pay to have them kept fresh from Memorial Day to Labor Day."

"Do you come often?"

"Yes, especially if I have reason."

He rubbed out a smudge on Grace's little marker. "I wish you'd told me before."

Maybe she should have. "I couldn't, Joe. Not the person I was."

"You're still that person, only better."

"It's been twenty-one years. I can't believe I still miss them so much."

"They gave you unconditional love. They're a part of you. Of course you miss them."

"You're right, you know," she told him, only just now realizing something herself. "And that love gave me the strength to endure all that came after. Through the love they gave me, they *are* a part of me."

"And you of them."

CHAPTER FOURTEEN

SATURDAY NIGHT, after dinner at a restaurant in downtown Lowell, Joe refused Elise's invitation to watch a movie with her in the family room. He didn't trust himself to sit with her that long and not think about touching her.

She didn't seem all that disappointed.

In his room, he put on his earphones, plugged in the MP3 player, grabbed the detective paperback he'd started and forced himself to read. He got through the crime—a brutal murder—without pause, made it past the witness interviews.

And then Detective Harris had a date.

Harris had a penchant for one-night stands. Always with a woman more beautiful than the last. And on this particular night, he was going to score.

Joe skipped a few pages, skimmed a couple more and found the morning after. Harris was hungover.

There was still beer in Harris's refrigerator— and a threatening note under his door. Someone intended to make sure that he didn't live to see another nightfall. He wouldn't know exactly when, or where, but his death had been plotted. He was going to walk right into it. There was no way out.

A crash sent Joe off the bed and to the door without removing his headset. Dropping the apparatus to the floor with the MP3 player he'd dragged along, he ran for the bathroom.

Elise had fallen. He just knew it. She was carrying around more than twenty extra pounds, all in front of her. Her balance was off.

"Elise?" he called, throwing the door open at the same time. He'd been so engrossed in fear, it never occurred to him that he was barging in where private business was conducted.

"Joe!" She grabbed a towel, pulled it against her, but not before he'd seen two of the most beautiful breasts he'd ever laid eyes on—in print or otherwise.

She had on the sweat shorts she wore to bed. And nothing else.

Joe stared at the towel, which concealed little of her breasts. And swallowed. There was something he should be doing. He knew that. He just couldn't think far enough ahead to get to it.

"I had a cramp in my calf and took a bath." Her voice was hoarse, as though her throat was as dry as his. "I tripped reaching for my shirt on the back of the door and knocked over the laundry bin."

"Are you hurt?" He was starting to breathe again.

"No."

Slowly, he raised his gaze to her face. Her eyes were wide, her mouth slightly open. Beads of moisture dotted her hairline. His gaze traveled back to the towel.

"I want to touch them." He couldn't believe he'd said that.

She nodded. "I know."

"You need to stop me."

"I covered them."

"It's not enough." His hands were shaking. He couldn't even think about what the rest of him was doing. In his sleep shorts, his condition would be obvious. If she looked.

"Maybe you should move out."

"Right now?"

"Uh-huh."

He thought about it. "I can't move out. Not for several more months. Maybe we should just do it once and get it out of the way so we quit thinking about it." *Obsessing* was a better term. He looked for something to do with his hands. His shorts were pocketless. He put his hands on the side of the sink and leaned on them. "You know…the grass is always greener on the other side. It's human nature to want what you can't have, but once you get it, you don't know why you ever wanted it to begin with. Maybe we just have to do this one time and then we can return to normal."

She didn't look convinced. "You really think so?"

"We've been together, what, fifteen years?"

"Just over."

"And we've never had even a hint of this problem before, so it stands to reason that we won't again. The close proximity created the situation and it's the age-old curse of wanting the forbidden fruit that feeds it. Once the fruit is no longer forbidden, our problem is solved."

She didn't openly disagree. She just stood there in the steamy room, her face flushed.

Joe's gaze returned once again to the towel. It had slipped slightly. Her nipples were a light gold—and larger than he'd expected.

He shifted on the sink, said, "Unless things have changed since last Sunday."

"Changed how?"

"You said I was turning you on."

"Yeah."

"Still?"

"Yeah." Elise licked her lips, allowing the towel to slip farther, and Joe was sunk.

"Can I have that?" He reached for the towel. She handed it to him. And straightened her shoulders.

With one hand still on the edge of the sink, he leaned forward, touching his lips to her nipple. He flicked it with his tongue, kissed, and then, with her moans urging him on, he gave in and did what he'd been dying to do for too long—took her nipple into his mouth and suckled her as though he had the right. As though she was his.

She pressed her shoulder forward, pushing herself more fully into his mouth.

Joe let go of the sink.

MUCH LATER THAT NIGHT, Joe felt a niggle of worry. Elise had just stirred in his arms, woken up, and her fingers were brushing lightly against his lower abdomen. She wasn't wearing any clothes. Neither was he.

At the angle she was lying, with her legs slightly spread beneath her rounded stomach, her crotch was in plain view. God, what a view. This was a whole new side to Elise Richardson—one that was so lush, so responsive and moist he couldn't believe she'd withheld it from him all these years.

The woman had a hair trigger. All he had to do was touch and her body spasmed with pleasure.

Her fingers moved lower, the back of one sliding along the length of his engorged penis.

How in hell was he ever again going to be able to return to normal? One look at her and…

"IT HAS TO BE HORMONES." Elise sighed late Sunday afternoon, half-asleep but feeling the tiny threads of need spreading between her legs.

Her nipples were tight and straining for Joe's touch, her fingers running along his lower back— a prelude to dipping lower.

"And they're contagious," he mumbled against her lips.

She'd made love with the man twice the night before. And when they'd first awoken this morning, tangled up in the middle of her bed, they'd done it again—without penetration this time as Joe was worried about her condition.

Dr. Braden had told her on Friday that she was still perfectly safe to have sex.

But the doctor probably hadn't meant multiple times in a twenty-hour period.

And at four that afternoon, they still hadn't been out of bed except to get his movie player, the paper and a couple of meals—all of which had been brought right back to bed.

He'd canceled his weekly basketball date with Kenny.

Samantha and Darin, who'd been locked out since the night before, periodically complained at the door.

Joe's lips slid past her chin, down her neck, over her chest, and she almost cried out in need and anticipation, waiting for him to capture her nipple again, suck on it until she exploded.

It took an embarrassingly short time.

"You're like this with all your men, huh?" he said, lifting his head to smile down at her after her orgasm.

"I wish," she said before she could think. Or even decide if she wanted to think. "I like sex, don't get me wrong," she said breathlessly, accepting his fingers between her legs, hugging him there. "But it's…you…oh…Joe…"

Giving up, Elise found his penis again, guiding it gently to her, inside her, and rode slowly with him, as, on their sides, gazes locked, they came together.

AT SIX, SHE LEFT HIM to take a shower. Joe offered to help. She declined.

"I'm pretty sure that 'one time to get it out of the way' means it has to end," she told him as she pulled a robe off the back of her bedroom door and covered herself.

With a pillow behind his head, he lay against the headboard, watching her. He'd pulled the sheet up to just below his belly button. The sight of that solid and flat stomach, the light scattering of dark hair growing there, almost had her climbing right back into bed.

But she had to be the strong one. The logical one. The one who set the parameters and reined them in. She always had been.

He saw the possibilities. She turned them into reality.

Or so she told herself as she stood alone beneath the shower, crying her eyes out.

"Please let it just be hormones."

SHE MADE EGGS FOR DINNER. Served them in the kitchen with the news on. And afterward she asked Joe to do the dishes, grabbed a pile of spreadsheets she'd brought home from the office, locked herself in her room with her cats, hungered horribly for Joe and prayed that by morning she'd be cured.

THE ROCKER THAT HAD BEEN on back order was sitting in a box on the side porch when Elise arrived home from work on Monday. She threw a frozen dinner into the oven, changed from her dress into sweats and opened the box. Taking the parts one by one from the porch to the nursery, she talked to her babies. Asked them to give her a knock now and then so she knew they were okay. Told them that she was going to learn how to stand back and let them try and maybe fail and that she'd always be there to pick up the pieces when they did.

And when the chair was gliding smoothly on its rails, she changed the sheets on her bed. On second thought, she switched out the comforter, too. If she'd had the energy she might have gone down to the local department store and bought four new pillows.

Joe was playing basketball with Kenny.

He didn't come home until long after she was in bed.

JOE TOLD HIMSELF NOT TO, but he showed up at Elise's office first thing Tuesday morning, shutting the door behind him.

"There's a rocking chair in the nursery."

She continued to type on her computer, staring at the screen. "I know."

"You should have waited for me."

"I didn't lift anything heavy. And I'm not an invalid."

Her refusal to look at him was driving him insane. At least, something was. He'd deliberately given her her space the day before—made goodwill calls on customers all day and spent the evening with his brother, who, if he'd heard about Elise and her pregnancy, didn't think to say anything about it.

Dropping onto the couch off to the side of her desk, Joe watched her fingers fly along the keyboard. She clicked her mouse. Typed some more.

Her hands were good at what they did.

"Don't you have work to do? A company to run?"

"Yes."

"There was a call from Michigan Local Banks. They want to know if we'll do full-time recruiting and how that will figure into their overall payroll percentages."

"I'll work up some figures and drop them off for you to look at. But be prepared, our competitor is on to them, too, so I'll write this in for no additional cost if it's going to break the deal."

She tapped a couple more times, her gaze moving up to the left-hand corner of her screen. And then she was off again, tap, tap, tapping until he wanted to yank the plug out of the back of her hard drive.

"Tamara sent us both a projection and work plan for the HR department, including estimated hours per task," she said. "Once you've had a chance to study it, I'd like to discuss it with you."

"Do you have reservations?"

"None."

"I'll bring it up as soon as I log on."

Still typing away, Elise nodded. What in hell was she doing? Writing a damned book?

"Look at me," he said.

She glanced. Quickly. Without turning her head. As though she were on the freeway, changing lanes in rush-hour traffic and sparing a second for whoever was in the passenger seat next to her.

"We have to talk about it," he said.

"No, we don't. Talking's what got us into trouble in the first place."

"It's not just going to go away."

"You said it would."

"So you just plan to avoid me until it does?"

"If that's what it takes." Her hair seemed spikier today. Her makeup more pronounced. She wasn't wearing any jewelry. Her shoulders were completely covered by a gray, short-sleeved tunic maternity dress.

"Why?"

Her hands dropped. "I'm pregnant, Joe," she said, looking at him. "Very soon, God willing, I'm going to have four children. You convulse at the thought of living with one. Children are unpredictable. They're chaotic. No matter what you do it's never enough. The job is unending.

"And I do not intend to raise them while having sex on the side."

Generally when she pointed out the flaws to a plan he was grateful. But then, that usually followed with ways to get around them.

"You're angry with me."

"No." Shoulders drooping, she leaned back in her chair, focusing on her computer screen again. "If anything, I'm angry with myself, but I'm not even sure that's accurate. I'm a realist, Joe. I see the pitfalls. Saturday night was a mistake."

Something inside him compelled him to speak out at that. "Saturday night *and* Sunday. You didn't seem to feel that way then. As I recall, you not only found satisfaction but—what were your words?— unspeakable joy, at times."

Her eyes, when she looked his way again, were wide open—and filled with sadness. "Lovemaking with you *was* unspeakably joyful," she said, her honesty settling the panic inside him, allowing him to really listen as she continued. "And I have a feeling I'm going to miss it for a long time to come."

Fine then. As long as they felt the same way, they could choose to do something about that.

"But I can live without it."

His neck started to hurt again.

"I can't live without B&R, you as a business

partner, or you as a friend," she went on. "And I can't live with sex on the side."

There was that term again. "Sex on the side." Where she'd gotten it, he didn't know. He didn't like it at all. But neither could he argue with a single thing she'd just said.

"I'm not moving out."

"I'm glad to hear that. I need you."

He needed her, too. Joe was only beginning to realize how much. But he was in no mood to tell her.

He headed for the door. "I'll see you at dinner."

"We're having scalloped potatoes and ham."

With his hand on the knob he turned to glare at her. "I hate ham."

"No, you don't."

Her expression was completely placid as she stared him down and Joe finally started to grin. He was a heel. A jerk. He was horny and frustrated and his condition was no fault of hers.

"You're right again," he said with a sorry chuckle. "And that I really *do* hate."

"I know."

Her last words didn't sound any happier than he felt.

ALMOST TWO WEEKS LATER, Joe wasn't feeling all that much better. Waiting while Dr. Braden examined Elise, he thumbed through an old edition of *Time* magazine, ran over the key points in his upcoming presentation to a commercial construction company later that afternoon and thought about the number of times he'd actually connected with his partner since the night and half the next day he'd spent in her bed.

That didn't take long. The answer was zero. They were working together, cohabitating, sharing meals and chores and news, but they were no longer lovers or even close friends. Not as far as he could tell. She was pleasant. He was pleasant.

And they didn't talk at all.

He missed her.

And even though he knew it had caused this horrible rift, he still wanted her.

"THE TIME HAS COME a little sooner than I thought."

Joe's skin went instantly cold at the doctor's first words past hello after closing her office door. Elise was going to have her babies now? They couldn't possibly be ready to sustain life on their own.

She sat beside him in front of Dr. Braden's desk, showing no signs of undue pain or discomfort. Her color was good. Only the droop of her shoulders, the smudges under eyes gave indication of anything wrong.

He'd thought she simply wasn't sleeping well.

"You want me to quit work," Elise said, sounding as though she'd just been sentenced to prison.

"I'm afraid so."

Joe glanced from one to the other, wondering what all the fuss was about. They'd known this was coming. Elise wasn't losing the babies. Life was okay for now.

"How about if I go part-time?"

"Why do you say it's time to quit?" he asked at the same moment.

Dr. Braden turned to him. "We've been monitoring Elise's blood pressure very carefully since before she was pregnant." The woman's explanation was businesslike, but with a hint of kindness. "Gestational hypertension is fairly common in multiple births, with almost a fifty percent occurrence rate, and can be deadly, both to the mother and the unborn children. It can cause seizures, visual disturbances and kidney failure in the mother, among other things."

Joe listened intently.

"The only cure is delivery."

At least there *was* one.

"Our goal is to allow these babies to remain in the womb as long as possible."

"Are you saying Elise has this condition, or just that we're being preemptive here?"

"My blood pressure is only slightly elevated," Elise answered him, still facing the doctor. "Not enough to be of concern yet."

"And sometimes the condition can exist without elevated blood pressure," Dr. Braden added. "I don't think we have anything to worry about, at least not yet," she continued. "But Elise's face is a little swollen and that's a common sign of gestational hypertension. There are other symptoms—higher protein waste levels and sensitive hyper-reflexia, knee-jerk, reaction—and so far Elise is testing normal for all of them. But with the swelling as a possible early indicator, if we want to be pre-emptive here—and I think we should be—it's time for her to stay home."

The doctor looked directly at Elise. "Full-time. So if the condition does fully develop, as long as we catch it soon enough, we have every chance of managing it."

Management. That agreed with him. "How do we do that?"

"When she's further along, that bed rest I mentioned the last time you were here. At this point, all you really need to worry about is a low-salt diet and plenty of peace and quiet."

"Can I work from home?" Elise asked.

"For now."

Elise seemed somewhat placated by that. Joe didn't care if she worked at all. He just wanted her alive.

CHAPTER FIFTEEN

"IT WAS THE SEX that did it." The idea had been growing on him all afternoon.

"No it wasn't."

"You were fine two weeks ago, having a perfect pregnancy, and the only thing you've done differently since then was spend a day in bed with me. I feel terrible."

They were eating at home Friday night. He'd grilled chicken—without salt. He'd have invited Kenny to join them, but Kate had kept her word and no one in his family knew he was staying with Elise.

It was much better that way. No hopes. No pressure. No ultimate disappointment.

"Well, don't. Having sex had nothing to do with it."

"You heard the doctor. You need peace and quiet, not multiple orgasms."

"Joe." She took a roll from the basket between them, ripped it open and gave him half. "I asked her about it, okay?"

"What did she say?"

"What's it matter? We aren't going there again."

"I'm not talking about doing it again," he assured her with utmost conviction. He wasn't going to do anything that might harm her—or these babies she so desperately wanted. "I'd like to hear what she had to say about what we've already done. I'd like the same peace of mind you obviously needed—and got." Honesty usually worked.

"I'm perfectly safe having sex right now." She cut a strip off the boneless chicken breast on her plate. "Assuming the hypertension doesn't develop, I could safely have sex for another couple of weeks." Another strip. "Because I'm at high risk for premature delivery, she'd like it if I didn't have orgasms past twenty weeks because they cause uterine contractions..." Strip number three. "And there's a small chance that they'd trigger preterm labor contractions." Sawing continuously, Elise started cutting the strips of meat into tiny pieces. "But generally that's not a concern until toward the end."

She wouldn't look at him. Just kept cutting. After she'd already told him everything. Unless...

Had she?

"What else?" Joe asked, on a hunch.

"There's no relevance to anything else."

"Humor me. Or I'll call Dr. Braden in the morning."

"She said that sexual tension can be particularly draining when hormones are overloading, and so, if anything, the orgasms might have helped as they release that tension and leave the body in a state of total relaxation." She had a plate full of tiny chunks of meat.

"You planning to feed that to the cats?" he asked.

She glanced at the meat on her plate, set down her knife, shook her head. She still didn't look at him.

And he thought about the two weeks looming between then and her twenty-week gestational age.

THE FOLLOWING MONDAY, when Joe left for work, Elise turned on the shopping channel and cleaned the cupboards in the kitchen, worked on the stuff they'd picked up from the office for her over the weekend, called the office several times and had a three-course dinner waiting when he got home that night.

On Tuesday, she turned on the shopping channel, got through the work Joe had brought home the night before in less than an hour and cleaned closets. She grilled hamburgers, without salt, for dinner.

On Wednesday, she cried for thirty minutes. And called Tamara, asking her new HR manager to meet with her there, at her house. She had a long list of things for the woman to bring with her.

Tamara was there by lunchtime with written reports from each of the employees. One of the new pay techs had made several errors that Elise found almost without looking. She should be there training the girl.

And some workers' comp forms hadn't been handled correctly. She fixed that with a phone call. And then asked how Tamara's mother was getting along.

"Her recovery's slow," the smartly dressed woman answered. "She's moving in permanently."

"How do you feel about that?"

"Okay." Elise knew a moment of sheer envy at the peaceful look that came over Tamara's face. "We've always been close. Probably because she gives me my space when I need it. And I hated living alone."

"I didn't like it much myself," Elise said, once again burying her nose in the folders her manager had delivered. She wanted to get through them in time for Tamara to take them back to the office with her before everyone left for the day.

"Are you and Joe getting married?"

Elise's head shot up. "Of course not!"

Tamara, sitting in Joe's seat at the kitchen table, glanced at Elise's stomach, which was growing by the minute. A little self-conscious in her shorts and cotton maternity top—certainly not professional wear—Elise put a hand on her protruding belly.

"He's not the father, Tamara, I promise. I really did do this on my own."

"I'm sorry." Tamara looked it, her long blond hair framing her frown. "It's just that pregnancies in single women are usually such a downer—and considered to be so much harder—and I can't believe any woman would actually choose to be in that position. I really thought you and Joe just said that to keep gossip down at the office until you decided what to do."

"Nope, I really chose it. Joe didn't even know about it until June."

"That's what he said, but when I heard from Angela that he's living here…"

"Only until I have the babies." Elise figured she probably should have been offended by her employees' nosiness, but all she could do was smile. Tamara, others at work, cared. She so badly needed to know that right then.

"Because I'm carrying quads, which I absolutely did *not* plan, I'm considered high risk. I was very likely going to have to spend the last months in the hospital if I didn't have someone here, just in case something goes wrong."

"And Joe just offered to move in?"

"We've been friends, just friends, since college." Elise tried to explain something she didn't really understand herself. Something she wasn't even sure was true after the Saturday night and Sunday that refused to go away no matter how hard she tried to banish them. "And it's not as though he had anything alive in his condo that would suffer from his not being there."

Tamara chuckled. She'd been around during the plant and cat episodes.

"And you honestly don't notice that he's drop-dead gorgeous? And kind, too?"

"Of course I know he's kind. Why do you think he's my best friend? I don't hang around with slouches, you know." She pretended she hadn't heard "drop-dead gorgeous."

"Maybe it's because you're pregnant and your hormones are messed up, but I could never live alone in a house with a man like that and not need to jump his bones."

Elise allowed Tamara to go on believing that pregnancy had robbed her of her sex drive and got back to work.

And for the rest of the day, took a small measure of comfort from what the other woman had said. Tamara was sure she'd have had the hots for Joe, too, if their situations were similar. Maybe she wasn't losing it, after all.

JOE CALLED THURSDAY, midmorning, to ask if it was all right if Mike, their IT guy, stopped by to set up her home computer on B&R's network. After she got over how stupid she'd been not to think of the solution herself, which took about two seconds, she joyfully agreed. And cried on her way to the bathroom where she quickly got herself in line, changed into navy slacks and a white maternity blouse, freshened her makeup and brushed her hair.

By afternoon, she'd be joining her world again—even if only technologically so.

ON FRIDAY, JOE BROUGHT HOME new cat toys for Samantha and Darin, claiming they'd been given to him by a pet store chain he was courting. Elise couldn't help but wonder how they'd know to give him two toys and have them be specific to cats, but she figured she'd be better off not pressing him. They were dancing around each other very nicely these days, but neither of them had ever been all that good at dancing. She didn't want to take any chances on slipping. Or causing him to do so. If either of them did, they'd likely both fall.

Which was why she readily agreed when he suggested a walk downtown to a restaurant for dinner.

"My mom asked about you today," he said after they'd ordered—fresh salmon for her, pizza for him.

"Did you tell her I'm now a stay-at-home?"

"Are you kidding? She'd have entertainment lined up for you every hour of the day if I did that!"

"And then she'd find out that you're living there."

"True. But, be honest, after a day or two of goofing off, you'd be tense about getting back to work."

She'd managed much better the latter half of the week—now that she had a system for keeping in constant touch with all of B&R's forms, files, records and staff.

"You know me too well." She sighed, but she was smiling. She felt good tonight. Good enough to approach the conversation she'd been meaning to have with him.

"Tomorrow's Saturday. I think you should go out on a date." She knew this was right. No one ever said right was easy.

"We're no longer in college, Elise," he said, eating the crust off the homemade bread that had just been delivered. "You aren't my cruise director anymore."

"You haven't needed one since college," she told him, proud of herself for the teasing smile she managed to give him. "It's not healthy for us, Joe, living like this. It's not fair to you. You like women. Spend time with them frequently. It's no wonder you…we…well, it's no wonder there've been some weird things going on. You need to get out."

Joe's frown was a little offputting. Sitting back, hands crossed at his chest—a very nice chest in the long-sleeved, casual denim buttondown he'd changed into after work—he said, "You talk as though I've got an entire harem just hanging around waiting for my call. Give me credit for having a little more couth than that."

"What about Melanie? You seemed pretty taken with her."

"I had lunch with her a few weeks ago. Neither of us seemed all that inclined to take things any further."

"Well, what about that woman you took to the gala at the state convention?"

"If I wanted a date, I could find a woman. In case you didn't notice, life's a little complicated right now. I'd rather not be any more duplicitous than necessary and I certainly don't want to pretend to a woman that I'm going home to my condo—or take her there—and then leave and come here. Nor do I want to explain to her why I'm living with you."

"So stay there."

"We've been over all that and I'm not getting into it again. This is September, Elise. You're due at the end of December. We can make it through four months."

Their food was placed in front of them. When the waitress left, Elise said, "I just think that your not dating is escalating the other…issue." She couldn't let it go. "And conversely, if you did date, it would diffuse it."

"I'm not going out on a date tomorrow night, Elise, or any other night until this is done."

Frustrated that he wasn't listening, and more so because a part of her was very fond of him for that, Elise dug into her salmon. "I'd take my own advice, but finding a guy who wants to ask me out in my condition and then settle for peace and quiet mostly at home, would be a little difficult."

"I'll do a lot of things for you, Elise, but dating when I don't want to isn't one of them."

She shut up after that and ate.

Thirty minutes later, Elise cradled her stomach as she waited at the table for Joe to find their waitress and pay the bill.

"What've you got, another six weeks or so?" a pretty woman with a sleeping baby in her arms stopped on her way out to ask.

"Not until December."

"You're kidding!" The woman's look of pained sympathy made Elise want to stay home and hide. "Is it twins?"

"Quadruplets."

"Oh, my gosh! Barney." She yanked at her husband's sleeve, getting his attention. "She's having four!"

"Damn!" The man looked at Elise's stomach. "Well, good luck to you."

His tone said she was going to need it.

"Yeah, good luck," his wife echoed, looking back one last time as she followed her husband out into the balmy September night.

"Ignore them," Joe said, coming up behind her. "They meant no harm."

"I know. Let's go home." She straightened, rubbing her back where it had rested against the hard chair back. Joe reached a hand down to her and without thinking, she took it.

And wished she hadn't. His touch was warm, reassuring, strong. And just as compelling as she remembered it.

ON SATURDAY, Joe went with Kenny to Ann Arbor to see a football game—University of Michigan against Central Michigan University. His brother drove—they left the Lexus at Kenny's condo—and on the way back, about an hour outside Grand Rapids, Kenny asked, "What's the matter with you today, bro? You got a deal working with someone who's to call today?"

They were a couple of hours from dark yet. He should be home by his usual time. "No."

"It's gotta be a woman then. A date you're hoping to confirm for tonight? 'Cause I gotta tell you, you've checked that damned cell phone so many times I'd think you were a horny school kid praying for the prom queen to call if I didn't know you better."

The prom queen had, in fact, hung all over Joe, and Kenny had helped him disentangle himself as tactfully as possible.

"Just making sure it's working," Joe said lamely. "I've had some trouble with it lately." More likely, the trouble was with him. And if he couldn't even go to a ball game with his brother and enjoy himself, he had to make some serious mental adjustments. Immediately.

"You want to stop for a beer and some pizza?" he asked, sliding his phone into the holder on his belt and vowing not to take it out again.

Unless it rang.

Then he'd look at it. And only then.

SUNDAY AFTERNOON, once he'd had his shower after shooting hoops with Kenny all morning, Joe found Elise in the kitchen, cookbooks and paraphernalia spread all over. She'd been leaving for the cemetery that morning when he'd headed out for his game.

"You having a party?" Hands in the pockets of his jeans, he glanced around at the counters. There were pasta, rice, loads of fresh veggies, tomatoes, onions.

His housemate shook her beautiful head, drawing his eye to the back of her neck. He'd kissed her there—two long weeks ago.

Two weeks ago right that minute, he'd been in bed with her.

"I'm making salad dressings, sauces, soup and a couple of casseroles—all without salt." She talked as she worked. "I found this article on the Internet about living with low-sodium diets. You don't have to hate your food, you just substitute other things for the salt. For instance, instead of garlic and celery salts, you use garlic and onion *powder.* And add other flavors with dry mustard, lemon juice, black pepper, things like that."

His mother had made a lot of food from scratch, too. But Elise, dressed in a pair of low-cut maternity jeans that hugged her legs and a long-sleeved flowing white blouse, looked nothing like his mother.

"Can I help with that?" He'd never once asked his mother that question.

"Sure." She handed him a knife and a bag of onions. "Start chopping."

Joe did. And was surprised to find that, despite the occasional burning in his eyes, the job wasn't nearly as onerous as he expected. He even forgot to turn on the pre-season National Football League game he and Kenny had bet on that morning until it was almost half time.

And when he realized that, when he saw himself becoming what he knew he didn't want to be—a man like his father, like Kate's husband, surrounded by chaos, at the whim of a houseful of people he'd never be able to please all at once, always exhausted, but never done—he finished the chopping and went to his bedroom.

JOE HELPED HIMSELF to seconds of the homemade casserole Elise served for dinner Sunday night. He'd finished his first helping mostly in silence. He turned on the game when he passed the little television on the way back to the table. She turned it off.

He wasn't surprised. She hated televised sports.

He wasn't all that hooked on them, other than their ability to help him relax—the drone of the announcer's voice put him to sleep on a regular basis.

"I think we have a problem with Michigan Local Banks," Elise said as soon as she sat back down. The company had all but signed with them. "This afternoon, while I waited for the casserole to cook,

I went over some paperwork Angela did last week, before I was online. She never filed for their workers' comp policy."

Joe swore. "It takes two weeks to a month to get that policy in place."

"I know."

"They were canceling their policy as of tomorrow, planning to sign with us."

"I didn't know it was that soon."

"I met with them on Friday. By the time I got home, I had other things on my mind."

To say the least. These days he had his business *partner* on his mind more than his business.

Elise's string of epithets wasn't quite as colorful as his, but just as effective.

"I'll call them first thing in the morning," he said. And between now and then he'd have to think of a way to approach his largest potential client with the news of a potentially dangerous error, at the same time instilling continued confidence in him and B&R.

"They should know that if I hadn't caught this," she said, "they'd have been without coverage."

"Because you *are* B&R and we look out for our clients, which is why we did see it in time." He went with her line of thought. It was ethical. And smart.

"I'm coming in tomorrow morning to speak with Angela."

It was the young woman's second major mistake in two weeks. And Elise hired, managed and fired all the staff—other than salespeople, who were his responsibility.

"I'll talk to her," Joe said, knowing he wasn't going to be nearly as effective as Elise would be. He wasn't as fully versed in the particulars of Angela's job duties as Elise was. But he wanted Elise to relax at home like the doctor ordered.

"I'm not going to stay long, Joe," she said, her plate empty as she sat back. "I'll come in mid-morning and be gone by lunchtime. I promise."

Michigan Local momentarily flew out of his mind.

She thought she was going to work. And she absolutely was not. They weren't risking her life. He studied her cheeks for a long moment, wondering if they were more swollen. He didn't think so, but then he hadn't noticed that they were to begin with.

"You're a grown woman," he said, choosing his words carefully. "And free to do as you wish."

"Thank you."

"However, as your friend and business partner, I'm asking you to please stay home."

She remained silent, although her look was stony. "I know you, Elise. You get to the office and you don't shut down. Your brain processes eighteen things at once, you see things that need to be done, things no one else is aware of. And as much as we need you there doing just that, B&R isn't worth risking on gestational hypertension. The company's important to us, yes, but if worse came to worst, as long as you're alive, we could always start another company."

It wasn't much, but it was the best he could do. There were things pushing at the edges of his conscious mind, things that he sensed were vitally important, but he had yet to realize fully what they were.

Things were changing. He knew that much. *He* was changing. But how it would all play out, for how long, he had no idea.

There was Elise. And then there were her impending offspring. And in between, an enormous barrier through which he couldn't see.

He wasn't any further into understanding himself than that.

"Dr. Braden would catch the condition long before it took my life."

"What about the babies' lives?" He stared at her, needing her to look him straight in the eye. "If the condition develops, it could force delivery before those kids are formed enough to survive."

He was shocked at the tears he saw in her eyes. "What?" he asked, frowning.

"Nothing." She wiped her eyes, shook her head, as though upset with herself. "These damn tears might be the worst part of this entire process," she told him. "Pain I can deal with, but I *don't* cry."

He didn't think it expedient to point out to her that apparently she did.

"There's nothing wrong with tears," he told her instead. "They're a healthy release of tension."

Like something else he knew—and had been trying adamantly to forget.

"They're annoying," she argued. "And a sign of weakness."

"If you're trying to sidetrack me, it's not going to work." He sat right where he was. "Tell me what made you cry."

Elise considered him for a long moment. "Just the idea that you care about these babies," she said slowly. "That anyone besides me really cares about them."

Stacking her plate on top of his, he carried both to the sink. Started rinsing.

"It's okay, Joe." She was just behind him, then beside him, and he hadn't heard her move. "I'm not insinuating in any way, hoping in any way, that your interest is anything other than avuncular. I knew before I started on this journey that I was going to be doing it alone. I *want* to do it alone. I just had no idea how much I was going to love them, or how all-consuming a parent's love for a child actually is. It felt good to know that while I carry around all this worry, someone else is here to share it with me. It felt good, just for the moment, not to be alone."

"You aren't alone." He could guarantee that. He loaded the dishwasher.

Elise wiped off the table. "I know. And I'm grateful."

"So you're going to stay home tomorrow, right?"

He waited by the sink, expecting her to say no.

It would be just like Elise. And there wouldn't be one damn thing he could do about it.

"Yes, Joe, I'll stay home."

Thank God for small favors.

CHAPTER SIXTEEN

"Aннн!" Elise shot up in bed just before midnight, clutching her bare calf, rubbing, trying to move toes that were completely stiff, tears running down her face. She'd never felt such sharp, immobilizing pain in her life.

"What is it?" Joe was beside her, his voice urgent.

"My leg." She fell to her side, her upper body writhing, her leg lying inflexibly against the sheet.

His hands were warm as they grabbed her leg. She concentrated on that contact.

"Bend your toes back and forth."

"I can't," she said, and cried out again when he did it for her. Her calf burned from the inside out, and she was sure the muscle had ripped. And then, as quickly as it had come, the pain was gone, leaving her leg limp and weak.

She needed to pull her nightshirt down farther. She stopped wearing shorts to bed when her waistline had expanded past the point of tolerating the elastic. But she was afraid to move, to reactivate whatever devil had hold of her body.

"What did you do?" She was lying in the middle of the bed, not quite facedown.

"You had a charley horse." Joe's voice was calm, reassuring. "If you'd played sports, you'd be painfully familiar with them."

"You've had them before?" Her lips brushed the sheet as she spoke. She wasn't as afraid of pain if she moved now. It was the man who'd saved her from that momentary hell that she now feared.

Or rather, her sudden reaction to him there, in her bedroom, on her mattress. Again.

"More times than I can count," he told her, and it took her a second to realize he was still talking about leg cramps. "They aren't serious, but while they last they're excruciating. The muscles tighten up and you just have to move them the right way to get them to loosen up. For calves, bending toes back and forth usually does it."

"But I wasn't playing a sport."

"You were standing on the hard tile of the kitchen floor most of the day, carrying around twenty pounds more than your limbs are used to supporting. That'll do it."

She nodded into the mattress, holding her breath until he left—now that he surely would be doing so.

His hand came down on her other leg—started moving across the muscles, kneading them gently and she sucked in air. "Just to make sure you don't get one in this leg as soon as you go back to sleep," he said, his voice slightly different. Softer. Huskier.

She lay completely still, her leg muscles softening into his touch, her lower stomach tightening. Think leg, she told herself. Relax. No more cramps. The furnace came on in the old house with a thud, and Elise jumped, jerking her leg, and Joe's hand slid down her ankle to her foot. He kept it there, massaging her arch and then all five toes.

With tingles speeding through her body, she almost bit into the mattress to keep herself from moaning. Could he tell her insides were squirming with desire again?

Her breasts, swollen and voluptuous, ached to be suckled.

Without a word Joe moved farther up her body, methodically finding every muscle, working each one firmly but gently—over her kneecaps, up her thigh and then around to her hamstrings. Elise bit her lip as long as she could, tried to put herself back in anatomy class, mentally going through each muscle group with him, but it had been too long since she'd met that undergraduate science requirement.

Her loud sigh shocked and then embarrassed her. He didn't miss a beat, as though he hadn't heard.

His fingers moved higher, working the top of her thigh, and she could think of nothing but her butt, tightening in anticipation, wondering if he'd massage her there, too. Glutes, they were called, she remembered. Would he touch them?

He passed over her butt to her lower back. But stopped before he'd really begun.

"Let's get you straightened out and moved up to your pillow," he said as he slid his hands under her arms to half lift her up the bed. Still mostly on her side, a requirement of her growing belly, Elise settled into her pillow, closed her eyes, willed herself to relax.

And all the while she traveled her body with him, inch by provocative inch, reveling in his current movement, predicting the next. When he moved up once more, just beneath her shoulder blades, would his fingers curve around her sides, touching her breasts?

Please, God. They were aching with need, her nipples budded against the mattress and pillow she was clutching.

Pulling lightly on her exposed arm, he worked her shoulder blade, and then did as much as he could with the other one, passing up to her neck and shoulders.

Elise could feel the knots he found, did her best to breathe into them, accepted the chills that passed through her—and prayed that he'd either stop or touch her more intimately.

Five minutes later, she was on the brink of begging.

"Turn over and I'll get the front of your shoulders and your other side."

She rolled onto her back. He continued to rub.

Closing her eyes, Elise moved her hand the briefest space and found his thigh, and moved it a bit more, around to his penis.

It was fully engorged.

He kept right on palpating muscles, up and down her free arm, her hands and each finger.

She held on.

He didn't acknowledge the grip.

But when he set her hand back down on the mattress beside her, his fingers found the edge of her nightshirt and pulled it up.

He was going to kiss her breasts. She just knew it. And couldn't wait.

The nightshirt stopped around her rib cage. Joe leaned over, not enough to pull out of her grasp, and she heard the click of the lotion container she kept on her nightstand just before the coolness of the liquid spread across her stomach. With a reverence she'd not expected possible, Joe's hands moved across her stretched skin again and again, lubricating, caressing.

She should have been embarrassed by her size. Instead, she felt the irresistible need to spread her legs.

And right then, from deep inside her, came the tiniest punch.

"What was that?" Joe jumped back out of her reach, snapping his hand away.

With a smile, Elise took hold of the hand he had in the air, brought it back down to her exposed stomach. "It's one of your nieces or nephews," she said.

No fatherhood. Only unclehood. She understood that. Was okay with it.

"It is?" He returned the other hand to her stomach, as well. "Will he or she do it again?"

"One or the other of them is at it pretty much all the time now," she told him softly. "But usually it's so faint I hardly notice. I'm told it will get much stronger as my pregnancy progresses."

"Tell him to do it again." Joe waited.

"Typical kids, they don't listen to their mama."

Joe's gaze raised to hers, held there. "Not this mama." His voice was almost a whisper. "No kid would dare ignore you, Elise."

She wasn't thinking about her kids. Her entire world was filled with the man sharing her bed.

As though he could read her mind, he lowered his mouth to hers.

The kiss was tentative, lips sealed, yet oh so erotic.

Scooting her hips to his thigh, bringing her lower body in as much contact with his as she could, Elise ran her tongue along the seam of his lips.

"We can't," he groaned.

"Yes, we can." She had to. "I'll bet my blood pressure's scaling the charts right about now." She found his penis again, stroked it. "I've got this tension tying me up so tightly I can hardly breathe."

He held his head inches from hers. "Elise—"

"You'll help me, won't you, Joe?"

She knew he wanted her—the evidence was impossible to hide. But he was frowning.

"Nothing's changed between us, I know that," she whispered. "I'm fine with that. You and me, like this, isn't permanent. It can't be. We have too much at stake to risk breaking up with each other. It's just for now, Joe."

Still he hesitated. Said nothing. She badly needed to know what he was thinking, but could hardly read his expression in the dim light. And desperation grew.

"I've only got six days until twenty weeks," she said more loudly, trying a chuckle that ended up more of a moan. "Please don't take too long to make up your mind here."

Her hand stilled.

JOE KNEW HE WAS SUNK. A strong man, he was capable of many things, but turning down Elise on the few occasions she asked things of him had never been one of them.

Taking the ends of her nightshirt, he raised it slowly, exposing breasts that had grown larger in the two weeks since he'd last seen them.

Grown larger without him. He had an instant when he felt as though he'd been robbed, and then the only thing he felt was a compelling need to find physical oneness with this woman. Now.

He massaged her breasts one at a time, cupping them in both hands, tending to them as he had to the rest of her body, honoring them, honoring her. And when it started to sound as though she was strangling, he bent, supping at first one nipple and then the other, arousing her, arousing himself.

Acting purely on instinct, he moved lower, kissing her stomach, caressing it. Who'd have thought the hard mass could be such a turn-on? "I've never made love to an obviously pregnant woman before."

"I was obviously pregnant two weeks ago."

He chuckled. Elise was rarely without comeback. He'd always liked that about her.

"I'm not sure what to do—how to go about this."

"Me, neither, though I know I'm dying to be touched down there."

Her knees were bent, her legs open. Joe found her with his fingers, faintly at first, drawing one finger around her before finding her core.

She'd found him again, too, and was mimicking his every move. Whatever he did to her, she did to him. His breathing became heavier. He considered the possibilities. And ten minutes later, they came together, their bodies connected, entwined, though he'd never put his hardness inside her.

They both fell asleep, Joe's fingers still holding her intimately.

ELISE ROLLED OVER when JOE left her bed in the morning, pretty sure he'd kissed her temple before he'd done so. Either that or she'd just dreamed he had. That gave her five to fifteen minutes to go to the bathroom before he hit the shower—depending on how deeply he dozed while his coffee brewed. She'd just close her eyes for another minute or two…

The bathroom door opening woke her more than half an hour later. Crawling out of bed, she made it to the door in time to see his naked back as he entered his room. He still had to put on his shirt and tie. She could make it to the bathroom and brush her teeth in time to say goodbye.

Not that she'd ever seen him to the door before. She wouldn't do so today, either, if not for the fact that he was going to be handling the reprimand of one of her employees.

He was talking to someone when she came out. Judging by the professional tone, she didn't think it was Samantha or Darin.

"I understand." He was holding his cell to his ear, and he turned his back when she appeared, still in her nightshirt, in the kitchen doorway.

"I understand," he said again, head bent as he rubbed the back of his neck. He might understand, but he apparently didn't like what he was hearing.

In dress slacks, a white shirt and black-and-white-striped tie, he was the picture of the stereotypical business executive, standing in *her* kitchen. While she was wearing a nightshirt.

She'd never lived with a man she'd had sex with. Wasn't sure of the protocol. But knew that whatever it was, it didn't apply here. Sex for her and Joe was not an ongoing thing. It was an aberration. A favor between friends.

"I appreciate that," Joe said now, staring out the window over the kitchen sink.

She sat at the table, stretching her nightshirt down over her knees.

"Keep us in mind if it doesn't work out."

Her heart sank. They'd lost a deal. Or a potential one. And she was afraid she knew which one.

"Tell me that wasn't Michigan Local."

Carefully, too deliberately, Joe clasped his phone back into the holder on his belt.

"It was. I'm going to work. See you tonight."

He took his keys out of his pocket and without so much as a wave in her direction, strode from her house.

IT WOULDN'T HAVE HAPPENED if she'd been at work, Joe thought. Even before they were born, children required all you had to give and then some. All you had to give was never enough.

He didn't feel calm—or kind—on the drive into the office. Six months of work down the drain. The biggest client he would have ever signed had just that morning gone with his competitor. They'd all had a late dinner the night before.

While he'd been in bed with his pregnant partner.

Angela Parks was at her desk, chewing on her bottom lip as she frowned at her computer screen.

"Oh! Joe! I didn't see you there," she said, quickly minimizing the screen as he stopped at the side of her cubicle. She giggled.

"Elise tells me you didn't file the Michigan Local workers' compensation papers."

"She knows? I was just getting it done."

"We lost the account this morning."

Her face drained of all color and the young woman looked like she was going to cry. Ruth Gregory walked by. A couple of pay techs were in surrounding cubicles. He should have called her into his office.

"Can you tell me what happened?"

"I meant to do it," she said, wringing her hands. "I thought I had. I'm not great at organizing, and Elise used to go over all key duties with me every couple of days. Lately I thought I'd been managing better than she'd have managed them for me. I don't know what happened…"

The girl was babbling. And while apparently a poor organizer, she was loyal, sharp and liked to please. His partner would have seen that. And had apparently decided that Angela's skills outweighed her weaknesses. That was why Elise was a good people manager and he was not.

"I'd be glad to meet with Angela three times a week if that'll help," Tamara said, appearing from behind Joe. "Things are still a little slow for me since we're just starting the department and only have a couple of clients."

Tamara Murphy, another Elise find. Joe tried to guess what his partner would do now. And drew a blank.

"Fine." He made the easiest decision, needing to get to his office before he took out his frustration on a twenty-five-year-old. "Let me know if you need any help," he added from the hall. He hoped to God he didn't hear from either of them again.

At least not for the rest of the morning.

IT WOULDN'T HAVE HAPPENED if she'd been at work, Elise knew. Her guilt hung heavily on her all morning as she logged in to the network that would put her online with work and perused B&R's payouts for the previous week. She'd promised Joe when they'd made these arrangements that she wouldn't call the office unless there was an emergency. Too much contact would cause stress, was his theory.

Judging by the tension running through her veins as she sat there wondering what was going on without her, she had an idea his theory was dead wrong.

But the man had sacrificed hugely for her—he'd put his entire life on hold while she lived hers. She had to honor his wishes wherever she could.

So she sat home. Worked. Rested. Felt her babies, talked to them. Took a hot bath. And tried not to feel completely dispensable to the rest of the world as she waited for Joe to come to her house for dinner.

Her house. Not his home.
She had to remember that.

THEY DIDN'T MENTION Michigan Local again. Joe
reported his conversation with Angela, including
Tamara's intervention—a situation that was con-
firmed the next morning via e-mail with her employees—and business went on. Joe had always
said that when you lose one deal, you go on to the
next, and based on what he had to say when he got
to the house each night, he was hell-bent on doing
just that. In the five business days of that week, he
made more calls than he'd made in all of the
previous month.

But each night, when the lights in her house
went out, he joined Elise in the bed in the small
bedroom next to the nursery. Sometimes he just
rubbed her back and legs. Sometimes his massages
were whole-body affairs. Every night he put lotion
on her stomach. They were intimate three times.

And spoke of the future not at all.

CHAPTER SEVENTEEN

"HERE'S BABY A..." the technician said as she used her laser pointer and mouse to separate the dark and light shadows on the screen. She found two arms and legs, measured the head circumference, counted ten fingers and toes, measured arm and leg-bone lengths.

Joe listened intently, studying the screen, and was actually able to discern eyes and nose and a tiny little...

"He's sucking his thumb!" Amazed, he glanced at the technician for verification of what he knew he was seeing.

"Yep!" the young woman, Sari, said.

"Elise, did you see that? Danny's sucking his thumb!" Joe glanced at his partner, on her back on the examining bed, and wished he could prop up her head, turn her on her side, anything to make her more comfortable. She was grinning at the screen, however, and didn't seem the least bit uncomfortable.

He knew she was. He'd been sleeping with her for six weeks, been helping to prop her stomach for the past two. She had a hard time breathing when she lay flat.

"Thomas's mouth is open," she said. He searched for Baby B. And found him only when the technician circled him. But he zeroed in on all the body parts quickly enough. Thomas was a little smaller than Danny. Dr. Braden had said size differences were normal.

Baby C, Ellen, weighed as much as Danny.

"She's going to be an athlete," Joe said.

"Or whatever else she wants to be," Elise added. Her smile was still wide, but the sweat on her upper lip told him she was having a hard time maintaining the position.

It was never enough. No matter what you did, how hard you tried, parents had to continue to give, to endure, beyond what they thought possible. He wondered if she was pretending not to care about the discomfort for his sake. She needn't have bothered.

Elise and the technician had to work together, changing positions, pressing on her stomach, to get Baby D, Grace, into full view. Distracted by his thoughts, Joe couldn't find the patches of white that designated arms and legs.

Sari was apparently having the same difficulty. She'd stopped talking. Stopped pointing and drawing. Her digital ruler moved. She clicked frames and saved them.

She prodded Elise's midsection again. And once more, apologizing when Elise winced.

"What's wrong?" Perspiration beaded on Elise's forehead as she frowned at the screen. "What is it?"

Sari shook her head. "Probably nothing. I'm just a technie and have no training for reading the results. Your doctor will be able to tell you anything you need to know."

"Something's wrong with Grace, isn't it?" Elise's voice rose, though she remained still as Sari finished up. "Tell me."

The young woman's face was straight. And white. Joe stepped forward. "Hey," he said to his business partner, holding her gaze with his own. "We're here together." He had to tend to her "alone" issues first or she'd panic. The past months had taught him that much.

Her gray eyes were smokier than usual as her gaze clung to his.

"We'll call Dr. Braden as soon as we leave here. Until then, try to relax. I'm right here and I'm not going anywhere."

Not until he got her through this pregnancy.

Hopefully with four healthy babies. All the care they'd taken, the doctor's orders they'd followed explicitly, the rest and peace and low-salt diet they'd provided had been enough, hadn't it?

Just this once?

"WE'LL DO ANOTHER ultrasound in a couple of weeks, but chances are we aren't going to know anything more until the babies are born."

Elise clutched Joe's hand, not caring how it looked, the false impression she might be giving, as she sat across from Dr. Braden's desk. Her other hand was beneath her rib cage, protecting her children.

She needed her mama.

"What's wrong?" Joe asked the doctor for her.

"Maybe nothing. It's important to keep that in mind."

It was serious, Elise was certain. She'd spent far too many years surrounded by doctors not to know when bad news was coming.

"Babies A, B and C are progressing nicely. Estimated weights coincide with hoped-for birth weights, bone measurements look good, heads are normal."

"And Baby D?" Her throat was so dry she could barely speak. "Is she alive?" Elise couldn't wait any longer.

"Yes."

"But there's a problem."

"The tech couldn't find a left arm."

Oh, God. She was so hot she was afraid she was going to throw up.

"That in itself is not all that uncommon at this point," Dr. Braden continued as Elise sat frozen in front of her. Joe hadn't moved, either. "With that many bodies in such a cramped space, the limb could easily be trapped beneath her."

Elise's face cooled. So it really wasn't a worry, yet. But wouldn't Sari have known that? While she might not see too many quad patients, she'd certainly done many multiples. Dr. Braden specialized in them.

"The real concern are her facial bones."

"Meaning what?" Joe's voice was clipped, his face, as Elise turned to him, completely stiff.

"She appears to be missing part of her left cheekbone."

"Is she going to die?"

Forearms on her desk, Dr. Braden set down the pencil she'd been toying with.

"As far as we can tell at this point, the possible deformities create no risk to the baby's life. Her heartbeat is stronger than Thomas's. She has the lowest projected birth weight, but it's still in range."

"I've never seen anyone missing a cheekbone." Joe, sounding confused, still held her hand.

"It's not all that common and it's not completely missing—if missing at all. Ultrasounds are not an exact science by any means. There's a lot they don't tell us."

"You think there's more?"

"There's always the possibility of internal problems, for any baby. For one with external problems, we worry a little more. But in the end, it's only worry. We can only tell so much until we actually get them here.

"There are other tests we could do to rule out problems, but I don't want to risk them this late in the pregnancy. It's not as though we could choose to do anything with the results at this point anyway."

"I thought we did all those and they came out fine," Elise reminded her, though she didn't actually believe that the doctor wasn't already fully aware, in far more detail than Elise was.

"We did. But conditions can develop as the babies develop."

"What did you mean? Do something with the results?" Joe asked.

"Selective reduction," Elise guessed. She wouldn't choose it even if there *was* time. As long as her daughter was alive, she would fight for her. Period.

"That, or any other kind of intervention that might make a difference," the doctor said. "Anything we do now could stimulate preterm labor and put the other three at too much risk."

Even in her womb, as in her childhood home the night of the fire, four siblings weren't equally safe.

"I'M NOT GOING TO LOSE Baby Grace again," Elise let Joe know, unequivocally, as soon as she was lying back against throw pillows on the couch in her family room. She'd thought about it nonstop on the silent drive home.

He'd offered to drive her by the cemetery on the way, but she'd declined. She hadn't been to the cemetery in weeks. Hadn't felt the pull to go.

He settled some pillows under her feet.

"She's going to grow up this time."

He shoved another behind her back.

"Isn't she?"

"There's no guarantee." His face was completely sober as he looked at her. "You do the best you can and sometimes it still isn't enough."

In that second, as she stared into Joe's eyes, it was as though she could see straight to his core. Something inside of her shifted.

"But it is, really, isn't it, Joe?" She felt an odd kind of strength. "By mere definition, you can't possibly do better than your best, so when it's done, you've done all you can. The rest is up to someone, or something, else. I couldn't do this alone, but I did my best, and then you were here to do the rest."

He stood over her, listening.

"Together we've done all we can."

"It still might not be enough."

She knew that. And if the unspeakable happened, she'd hurt like hell, and she'd survive. She always did.

"I CALLED THOMAS this afternoon."

Joe held still in bed that night while she settled her stomach against his bare back. He'd toyed with the idea of calling Kate to come stay with her. His sister would gladly have done so.

But in the end, he had to be here. He'd given his word. He'd keep it. And on January first, he'd be free to go.

"You told him about Grace?" he asked when he realized she was waiting for some kind of response from him.

"I asked him about replacing a missing cheek-bone."

Of course. The man he'd yet to meet was a gifted plastic surgeon.

"What'd he say?"

She moved her legs, curling them into his, until all that separated her skin from his were his recently purchased pajama bottoms.

"It all depends on how extensive the deformity is, of course, but there's much that can be done. Bone grafts, implants, all kinds of things."

Because when you were Elise, and you did all you could do, someone else was there to do the rest.

He hoped.

"I REALIZED SOMETHING ELSE today." Elise's words brought him from the brink of sleep.

"What's that?"

Joe resisted turning over—only because he knew how hard it was for her to find a comfortable position. And because if he did, he'd want to touch her in ways that were too dangerous these days.

On many levels.

"Knowing that Baby Grace might be deformed doesn't in any way change the connection I feel to her."

"You thought you'd love her less?" That surprised him.

"Of course not!" Elise's breath was warm and

wispy on his neck. "But ever since I found out the sex of the babies, since they've been named, I've had a sense of who they are. When I think of Grace deformed, that sense of who she is doesn't change. I think of the being I know her to be possibly dealing with a hardship, but there's no change in who her spirit is. Does this make any sense at all?"

Joe did turn then, slowly, a hand beneath her stomach as he did so. "It makes complete sense," he told her, their faces close enough that he could see her eyes. "I'm not sure how many people would be struck with the same insight, but for you it fits perfectly."

"Why for me?" She frowned and he ached to smooth her brow with a kiss. He'd never have another friend like Elise Richardson.

"Think about it," he told her softly, wanting her to figure this one out on her own.

She lay there silently, staring at him.

"Do you remember the explanation you gave me when you told me you were pregnant?"

"Not word for word."

"What was the gist of it?"

One of the babies kicked against his hand— Grace, he chose to think—and Elise didn't even seem to notice.

"That I had no sense of self, of family or belonging."

"What else? Specifically to do with the fire and the result of the years you spent in the hospital afterward."

"I bear no resemblance to my real self," she said as though that was a given.

"Uh-huh." He waited, watching her changing expressions.

"But the person I am, the spirit that makes me me, is always there, no matter what I look like." The realization came slowly, gaining in momentum.

Very gently, careful not to arouse inappropriate feelings now that they were beyond that point in their relationship—and most importantly in her condition—Joe kissed her.

"I can't believe it took my love for my daughter to help me see that about myself," she breathed when he pulled away.

"Sometimes another perspective is all we need."

"You think?"

Sometimes he did.

THANKSGIVING CAME AND WENT quietly. Joe's mother urged him to invite Elise along with him for dinner, but Elise hadn't been up for traveling. His mother, still not aware that Joe was staying with Elise, had then insisted that Joe come by for a care package and share dinner with Elise as no one should be alone on a holiday.

He didn't argue.

SHE HAD TO HAVE a Christmas tree. At almost fifty pounds more than her normal weight, Elise couldn't possibly climb on a ladder to decorate one—as she'd done every year since she'd been on her own—but she at least had to have one. Trees were a symbol of life, of hope, of childhood and magic and dreams coming true.

She had to have one.

From the sofa in her family room, she called Colby, her IT guy at work, the Friday after Thanksgiving and offered to pay him a hundred dollars if he'd have a tree at her house before Joe returned from watching a football game with Kenny at his brother's condo.

JOE WASN'T TOO PLEASED when he got home and saw the big tree in her living room.

"Tell me you didn't go get this."

"I didn't." She was leaning against the archway between the living and dining rooms, holding her lower back. It had been hurting more than usual all day. "Colby brought it."

"You can't decorate it."

"I know. I just needed to have one."

"Are your decorations still under the steps in the basement?"

He and Kelly had been over one year to help her with her tree. Elise had invited them after Kelly had told her that they never had a tree. Joe thought they were too much bother for too short a time.

"Yes." Joe had contributed the pizza and beer that night a few years before. He hadn't, as she recalled, hung even one ornament on the tree.

By dinnertime, the tree was a glowing mass of color, lights and glitter. He'd done the top—talking about the thumbs-up call he'd received that morning from the new nationwide restaurant chain he'd been courting. She'd done the bottom—double-checking with him that all forms had been processed and all personnel had been told exactly what to do for him to make the deal transition smoothly. And together, with pillows propped around Elise, they ate low-sodium vegetable soup with salt-free crackers on the living-room floor.

THE FOLLOWING WEEK, Joe came home to several festively wrapped packages under the tree.

"You went out shopping? In this weather? With the holiday crowds?" Was the woman hell-bent on driving him crazy? Didn't she see how hard it was to leave her in this condition at all? How much he worried every single minute he was apart from her? And most of those when he wasn't?

She was so huge she was off balance much of the time. And the things that could go wrong at this stage—the five lives that could be lost...

"Calm down, Joe," she said now, dryly. "I watch the home shopping channel, remember? These things have been arriving for days."

He was never going to make it to her delivery date.

ON SATURDAY, DECEMBER 9, gestational age 32 weeks, Elise went into labor. She'd been in the hospital for almost a week, fighting gestational hypertension.

"I'm on my way," Joe told her, cell phone to his ear as he left Samantha and Darin in the kitchen waiting for him to fill their bowls with the can of dinner he'd just opened.

"You don't have to come, Joe. They'll call…" Her voice was weak and he stepped on the gas.

"You don't think I came all this way to miss the grand event, do you?"

Though he'd visited her every night that week, they'd never discussed the actual birth—other than in terms of the ninety-four percent chance of C-section delivery and requisite recovery time.

There was just no way he could leave her to go through this alone.

No way he could sit around and wait to hear that she was all right.

"Thank you."

"Are you crying again, woman?"

"No." She sniffled.

"Okay, good. Just checking."

He continued talking inanities with her until he'd reached the part of the hospital where he had to turn off his cell phone.

SHE WAS NO LONGER in her room. Joe, rounding the corner to see the empty bed, panicked. He turned urgently back to the hall, searching frantically for anyone who could direct him. He grabbed an orderly who knew nothing about Elise, but who knew enough to find him a nurse.

The woman, a weekend fill-in, assumed Joe was the father of Elise's children and had him garbed in blue scrubs and a mask before he could tell her he wasn't. Down the hall from the sleeping rooms, past the birthing rooms, she held open a silver door.

"Right in there."

The room reminded him of the set of a local morning television show he'd been on when he'd done a professional employees' organization info-mercial. Rapidly moving and focused personnel all close to wired machines, busy doing stuff he knew nothing about.

And monitors everywhere.

"Joe, right over here." Dr. Braden came up behind him. "She's just been prepared for surgery."

On the far side of the room, past two crib-looking things on wheels, Elise was semi-propped up in swaths of green cloth. A green elasticized cap covered her short dark hair.

"Hi." She smiled wearily.

He found her hand, took hold of it. He wasn't moving until she was safely through this.

"They're doing a cesarean."

He'd figured as much. "Everything okay?"

"So far."

"Everything's going to be just fine."

She nodded.

"It'll be quick this way." Dr. Braden had discussed the process with them. They didn't have to worry about pushing, or breathing. They just had to hang out and let the professionals do their jobs. "Once we get going, it'll only be a couple of minutes before you're holding your babies."

"I'm scared, Joe."

Her fear fed his.

And his job was to be calm. Convincing.

"My friend told me once, not too long ago, that we do all we can and then someone else will do the rest," he said. "Well, you've done all you can, and now it's time for Dr. Braden to step in."

"I know." She licked her lips.

Joe looked for the little plastic pitcher of water that had been beside her bed all week, and, not finding it, requested one. He was given a cup full of ice chips and told he could only rub them along her lips. She wasn't to consume anything until after surgery.

Sheets were moved, exposing only a thin portion of Elise's lower abdomen area. A tray of utensils appeared and Joe turned his back.

"What if she doesn't have an arm?" Elise whispered.

"She'll learn to do things with one hand."

Babies were about to be brought into the world only a foot behind him. Elise's babies. The children he'd spent the past six months helping her prepare for.

Adam Fallow's children. Or one of the other four donors.

"Thank you, Joe. For everything. These past months…"

"Ssshhh." He brushed tears from her cheek. "You've been taking care of me for fifteen years, partner. And I'm counting on you to continue doing it for the next forty-five."

At work.

"I love you."

He wasn't sure he'd heard her correctly. And then had the idea that she'd been speaking to someone else. Or was out of her mind.

Elise wasn't the sort of person who said, "I love you."

"I didn't mean to say that." Her voice was husky, weak. "You're the first person I've said that to since I was eleven years old."

He couldn't believe this was happening. Now. In the middle of a surgical birthing room with her stomach being plundered, surrounded by God knew how many people.

"So you didn't mean it."

Why weren't babies crying?

"Oh, I meant it. I just didn't expect to tell you."

He had absolutely no idea what to do. Or say. And was bothered by the lack of baby sounds.

"It's good for friends to love each other, don't you think?"

"Yes." An answer he knew.

"You're the best friend I've ever had."

They must have given her more than the local

anesthetic that had been discussed earlier in the week.

"Same here."

"Joe, I feel kind of funny…."

"Blood pressure's dropping."

A male nurse pushed Joe aside, reaching for the oxygen mask above Elise's head. Someone else ushered him rapidly out of the room, but not before he heard the nurse's urgent words.

"We're losing her!"

CHAPTER EIGHTEEN

JOE PACED THE HALL in front of the family waiting room on the maternity floor for about two minutes. And then, in a cell-phone-safe area, he dialed his mother's number.

"Elise is in trouble."

"Where are you?"

He named the hospital.

"We're on our way."

KATE WAS THERE. And Kenny. His mother and father sat on either side of him. The rest of his siblings were at home with their kids, but sitting close to the phone.

They had the waiting room to themselves. Someone had decorated it for Christmas since he'd last seen the place several days before. A small tree sat on the corner magazine table. Red and green metallic garlands, hung from the ceiling, ran all around the room. Handmade childish renditions of paper ornaments adorned the walls.

"I can't lose her."

"God's will is stronger than yours, son."

"Hard to believe, huh?" Kenny quipped, then quickly sobered.

It had only been half an hour, but Joe felt like he'd been wrapped in cotton for days. "I can't imagine life without her in it."

"I thought you guys were only business partners," Kenny said.

"We are."

"Well, you sound more like you're lovers."

"Kenny!" Kate slapped his thigh.

Joe went cold. She'd said she loved him. And he'd lost his chance to tell her that he loved her, too.

"We've been together a long time." He aimed the lost words at his brother.

He loved her. No wonder the idea of Adam Fallow stepping in had grated so much.

"I kept waiting to hear babies cry, but there wasn't any sound."

"You were with her?" His dad's words rang with his surprise.

"Joe's been living with her." This from Kate.

"You have?" His mother turned to study him.

"You have?" Kenny's mouth fell open.

"Just until the babies come. She couldn't be alone at night." The reason sounded weak, but he stood by the decision he'd made. "Kate's taking over afterward."

"You're just going to move out and leave Elise there?" His mother sounded none too pleased.

He glanced at his watch. Thirty-five minutes. What was taking so long?

Was she even still alive? Oh, God.

"You'd move out on that babe?" Kenny asked.

"In case you guys missed it, she's in there giving birth to four kids." Please, God, let that be so. "All at once. How well do any of you think I'd do there? This is *me* we're talking about. Surely you all remember how I was when the four little ones came along in *our* family?"

Why wasn't someone coming to get him?

"How was that, Joe?" Clara asked. "As I recall, you were everyplace I needed you, when I needed you. I used to brag to my friends that you were going to be a great father some day."

Where was Dr. Braden?

"You had the patience of Job," Kate said. "I remember walking into the family room one time and seeing you on the floor, your head propped up in your hands as you watched TV, and one of the little ones, I forget who right now, was sitting on your back pulling your hair. You kept swatting at that little hand, but you were so tolerant. You just lay there, watching cartoons."

He didn't remember that at all.

And what about Baby Grace? Had they saved her? Did she have both arms? And a strong heart?

"You sure made me look like a slump," Kenny said. "'Kenny, we can't play ball now, we have to get home,'" he mimicked. "'Kenny, hurry up, the kids'll be waking up and Mom'll be mad if we aren't there....'"

He did remember that. The basketball and baseball games he'd missed. The pressure, the hurry, and still, more often than not, in spite of his attempts to prevent it, the house would be in total chaos by the time they got home from school.

He'd give them five more minutes to come out of that delivery room and then he was going in. It was inhuman what they were doing to him, making him sit here like this not knowing if any of the five people he'd spent six months caring for were even alive.

"I hid out in the attic," he said, having no trouble dredging up the memory, since it had happened so often. "You all know that. Eventually you guys let me move up there."

"Because you seemed to like it there so much," Edward said. "You gave so much of your time to the family, we thought you deserved some time to yourself."

He gave so much to the family?

"Every night when I went to bed, you and Mom were so tired you could hardly see straight, and there was still someone whining at you to do something, get something, and I'd feel like a heel for leaving you to it, but I couldn't wait to get away."

"That was our responsibility, Joe, not yours," Clara said, her voice as firm.

"One we wanted," Edward added. "Sure we got

tired, but when we went to bed at night, our hearts were full."

"You were just a boy," Clara continued when his father finished. "Getting away wasn't a prize, but a right. I thought you knew that."

He didn't know what he knew anymore. The four people facing him had been with him all those growing-up years. In that house, with all the chaos. And their memories were so different from his, he thought they'd all lost their minds.

The only other option was that *he* had. And he wasn't equipped to consider that right now.

"Joe?"

He jerked to his feet at the sound of Dr. Braden's voice.

"She's asleep but you can sit with her whenever you're ready."

"She's okay?" He was already at the door.

"Yes." She glanced at the group of people she'd never met. "She's going to be just fine."

He almost sank to the floor. Thank you, God.

"And the babies?"

"I'll let you see for yourself, if you'd like to come now."

With a last glance at the members of his family, all of whom were smiling and nodding at him to go, he headed down the hall with the doctor.

THE NEONATAL UNIT was in another wing, but on the same floor. Still wearing scrubs, minus the cap,

Joe prepared himself for whatever he might find at this short journey's end.

Dr. Braden stopped at a big window in front of the two criblike affairs he'd seen in the delivery room more than an hour before. Except now they held four of the tiniest bodies he'd ever seen.

"Do all those tubes and things hurt?"

The doctor shook her head, and all Joe could do after that was stare as something settled deep inside of him.

They were breathing. All four of them.

They all had ten fingers and ten toes....

"Grace has her arm."

"Yes, she does."

The doctor was a busy woman, but she didn't seem any more inclined to leave their vigil than Joe did.

He looked for the missing cheekbone.

"Which one is she?"

"Baby D, over there."

The one with the most perfect, round little baby face he'd ever seen.

"So she's fine."

"As far as we can tell right now, they all are." The woman talked about scores and birth weights, heart rates and sucking skills. All Joe could see was the miraculous outcome of all of Elise's hard work.

His partner had really done it this time.

THE FIRST THING Joe did when he entered Elise's private room was go over and kiss her. Lightly.

"Joe?" Her eyes opened.

"Yeah."

"What happened? Where am I? Is it over?" Her voice rose with panic as she attempted to sit up.

"Dr. Braden's already been in and spoken with you, but she said you probably wouldn't remember."

Her hands drifted down to her abdomen. "Where are they, Joe?" Tears filled her eyes. "Something happened to them, didn't it?"

"Shhh," he said, just as he had hours before, wiping away her tears. "You need your eyes clear to see this."

He pulled out his cell phone, opened it and held it in front of her face, showing her the new background image as of fifteen minutes before.

"That's them? Those adorable little things are my babies?" She was crying again.

"And you chided me for buying a camera phone."

"Oh, Joe." She pulled the phone back. "They're really mine?"

"They really are. I read the tags, just to be sure. Baby A is right here, and with him is Baby B. Ellen is right there. And here's Grace."

He heard the proud papa tone in his voice and didn't care. He was, after all, the children's honorary uncle.

"She has two arms."

"And a gorgeous little face, wouldn't you say? Just like her mama."

Elise released a sob. And then winced.

"What's the matter?"

"I think I just pulled my stitches."

"Should I call for someone?"

"No." She lay back and grabbed the phone again. "I just can't laugh too much in the next day or two."

"WHEN CAN I SEE THEM? For real, I mean?" As exhausted as she was, as sore, Elise couldn't stand to remain in the bed when her very own children were right down the hall.

"In just a bit," he assured her. "If we can't get you into a wheelchair I've already received special permission from Dr. Braden to wheel your bed down to the window. They're working on the babies right now."

"Is something wrong?"

"Nope. Just normal checks of things I didn't even know they *could* check. As you saw, they're all breathing on their own, and that apparently was the biggest hurdle. If all goes well we should be able to take them home in time for Christmas."

We? Her eyes met Joe's, but she didn't say anything. The day was too perfect to muddy it with reality.

ON SUNDAY, two by two, Joe's entire family and the employees of B&R PEO came by the hospital to wish Elise well, drop off gifts and take a peek at the babies. They were still in incubators, two in each to simulate the company they'd kept in the womb. The night before, as she'd lain in her bed outside the neonatal nursery unit watching her children sleep, Elise had cried far more than her babies had. Later that afternoon, after she rested, Elise was going to be wheeled into the room so she could touch them for the first time.

When it was time, Joe pushed her chair down the hall to the nursery.

"I haven't held a baby since I was eleven."

"Well, you're about to get lots of practice." Joe's cheerfulness from the day before hadn't worn off a bit, even after all the sleep he'd lost, staying with her half the night.

"Two can go in at a time." She told him what Dr. Braden had said earlier when she'd stopped by on her rounds. "You want to come?"

"I'll watch from the window."

She'd expected that answer.

"COME ON IN." The nurse, Tanya, opened the door for them. "They're expecting you."

Joe held the door. "You want to take her chair from here?"

"You aren't coming?" Tanya didn't wait for Joe to answer. "Of course you are. There're four little ones in there and four arms out here. I think that works out just about right."

Elise started to protest, then stopped when Joe pushed her through the door, following Tanya over to the twin incubating beds.

"Who wants Baby D first?" Tanya asked.

"I do." Joe was faster than Elise. "But give two others to Elise first. I'll watch."

"I'll take the boys," she said, eyeing her daughters with awe and envy. And then, as Tanya placed one tiny body in the crook of Elise's right arm, she had eyes only for Daniel. He might be the largest of her crew, but at four pounds one ounce, he wasn't much bigger than her fist.

"What about the tubes?" From her vigils at the window, she knew what most of them were for.

"I've got them taped," Tanya said, reaching back into the bed again. "Just be mindful and you'll be fine."

She turned back, her expression soft as she looked at the infant in her arms. "Here's Baby B."

Thomas. My littlest love. Only three pounds eight ounces. Elise accepted him—and he opened big blue eyes to stare straight at her. She glanced up with tears streaming down her face, just in time for Joe to snap a picture.

Two minutes later, he was in a rocker opposite her, with a baby girl in each arm. She wished she had a camera, but knew she wouldn't need one for this.

The sight of her partner, sitting in a rocking chair in the neonatal nursery with her daughters in his arms, was something she was never going to forget.

JOE STAYED UNTIL MIDNIGHT on Sunday night to watch the eleven o'clock feedings. Each baby had to learn how to breathe, suck and swallow. As soon as that was accomplished they could go home. Elise was due to be released in the next day or two, assuming her incision continued to heal as nicely as it had so far.

And on Monday morning, after feeding two lonely cats who continuously brushed against his legs as he stood at the counter preparing their food while his coffee percolated, he left for the airport. He wanted to be at the hospital by nine for the next feeding and he had an important errand to run first.

He recognized the older couple almost immediately as they came down the hall past the security checkpoint. He brushed his sweaty hand against his slacks as he stepped forward. He couldn't ever remember being so nervous to meet another human being.

"Dr. and Mrs. Fuller?"

The man was tall and thin, with a full head of white hair. His wife, Elizabeth, was round and gracious and couldn't seem to stop smiling.

"Thank you for coming to pick us up," Dr. Fuller said, shaking Joe's hand. "Elise has mentioned you. You two are in business together, aren't you?"

"For more than ten years," Elizabeth put in. She scrutinized Joe. "Are you married?"

"No, ma'am."

"And you've been staying with Elise?"

"Yes." He felt heat creeping up his skin as he

considered some of what he and Elise had done during those months together.

"She still doesn't know we're coming?" Dr. Fuller asked as they waited for their baggage.

"Nope." Joe had taken their call early Sunday morning on Elise's cell, which he'd brought home to charge. "I wanted to surprise her."

"I can't wait to see those babies!" Elizabeth beamed. She was a pretty woman. A peaceful woman.

"You two never had any children?"

"We tried, but it wasn't to be," Elizabeth said. "But we had Elise. What a dear, dear child she was. In more pain than most of us could have endured, and she never complained."

"Did she tell you about finding an article that had been written about her on my desk?" Thomas Fuller asked, hands in his pockets as he rocked back and forth on his feet.

"No." But Joe hoped the doctor was going to tell him.

"I'd won an award for my work at the plastic surgeons convention. There were pictures of her face—in all stages of her ordeal. I'd never told her I'd published them."

The man's pain was obvious, which made it a little easier for Joe to continue to like him.

"She was shocked. Hurt," Thomas Fuller continued. "But she never held it against me. That girl has the ability to see inside a person and love what's there, no matter what's on the surface."

Joe saw clearly now what a jerk he'd been all these years, sharing much of his life with an angel and not seeing her wings.

LIFE WAS INCREDIBLE. Brimming with wonder. Full.

Elise sat in her hospital bed Tuesday afternoon, listening while Thomas and Dr. Braden discussed her as though she wasn't there. Joe had taken Elizabeth down to the nursery while the doctor made her rounds.

"Excuse me," she finally said, smiling. "Can I go home now?"

"I don't know. What do you say, Doctor?" Dr. Braden looked at Thomas. "Can we trust her to follow orders?"

"You can trust that if she doesn't she's probably going to be just fine anyway," Thomas said. "This girl's a survivor. The one thing I've learned about her is never to underestimate the strength of her will."

Elise wanted to hug him. She still couldn't believe he and Elizabeth were really here.

And couldn't believe that Joe, for the second day, was hanging out at the hospital and not at B&R.

She wondered if what Thomas had said was really true. That if she wanted something badly enough, she'd get it. She thought of B&R and how successful it was. She thought of her babies, all beautiful and healthy.

It must be true.

THE FULLERS, staying in a room at a local bed-and-breakfast, were in town another day after Elise was released. And then it was just Joe, who was sleeping in his own room in her house again, watching over her and taking her to and from the hospital to visit her babies. She decorated the babies' warming beds and the walls in front of them with Santa Claus faces and brightly colored ornaments, read to them, learned how to care for them, staying long hours because she didn't want to miss any feedings.

On doctor's orders she had to miss the middle-of-the-night ones, and so she pumped milk to cover the feedings. She was able to breast-feed all four of them by the end of the first week, though Thomas's meals were still being supplemented by tube feedings.

On Saturday, Ellen was put on medication for reflux. And on Sunday the neonatal team called for a renal ultrasound on Danny—suspecting possible blockage. Baby Grace had gained the most weight—six ounces. Thomas was still on ultraviolet light for jaundice, and Elise was exhausted.

"You should go home," she told Joe just after six Sunday evening. "You've been here all weekend and you have to work tomorrow."

They were sitting in the neonatal waiting room eating sandwiches from the vending machine. Christmas lights, the tree and decorations, gave the room a warm glow.

Joe supposed she was right. Someone had to do laundry. He was wearing his last clean pair of jeans. It was less of a problem for Elise—she was still in sweats—but she had to be getting low on underwear and bras.

"I have to come back and get you anyway," he said. She'd asked about the office every evening the previous week when he'd come to the hospital from work. Was somehow keeping up on what was going on there as well as in the nursery.

"Then I'll leave now, too," she said, standing.

"And miss the eleven-o'clock feedings?"

"I pumped enough to cover for me."

"Thomas does better when you feed him directly."

Besides, he wanted to give Ellen her bottle. He had a system with her, a few tugs and he pulled the bottle out, giving her more time to swallow so she didn't gulp air at the same time. But you had to time it just right or she'd cry and then the entire feeding became a struggle.

She spit up less when he had her.

"I'll be fine," he told Elise, not as amazed as he might have been to know the words were true.

"Joe—"

"It's okay, Elise."

She sat back down, glaring at him.

She was beautiful when she frowned, her dark hair framing the expression. Maybe because her eyes became smokier.

"I've discovered something about myself," he said. Now probably wasn't the place and time for this, but she'd given him the opening. And he owed her. Like Thomas had once, he'd hurt her. He'd been so hell-bent on the life he'd mapped out for himself when he was a kid, when he was blind to so much, that he'd closed himself off from the truth.

He knew that now.

"What's that?" Her grin was almost playful, as though she didn't expect much of a revelation.

"I'm an idiot."

She laughed. "I hate to break it to you, Joe, but your big discovery is a bust. There's nothing stupid about you."

"There is. Was. I've spent my entire life running from something that didn't exist, and missing everything I wanted in the meantime."

"Such as?"

"A full life. Love. Sharing. Family. I have such a big family I took it all for granted. Figured the family was already there so I didn't need to create another one."

Her silence was a bit unnerving.

"I put all this pressure on myself as a kid," he went on, "thinking I had to take care of my mom and the little ones, when in reality, my mom was there to take care of me. She was always so busy, I didn't figure she had time for me. A lot of days I didn't think she even noticed me except when I was there to relieve her burden."

Now Elise spoke. "I can't believe she really felt that."

"Well, here's where the idiot part comes in." He wadded up the plastic wrap from the sandwich he'd consumed, put it back in its hard plastic container and set them both on the table. "I *did* believe it. I knew she loved me. But I honestly thought she was so overwhelmed with children she couldn't be there for me."

"Middle child syndrome."

"Maybe." He'd like to think there was some valid basis for his trek so far off base. "What I've recently discovered, and should have figured out twenty years ago, was that she was thinking of me all along. Here I thought I was escaping to the attic, feeling guilty for doing so, when in reality, she and my father told the other kids to stay away from there—it was my special place and I wasn't to be disturbed."

"And you never knew that?"

He shook his head. "We see what we expect to see."

Her reply was slow in coming, drawn out. "Yes, we do."

"This past week, probably even before that, I found that I go to bed exhausted, but when I wake up in the morning, even if I've only had a few hours' sleep, I'm energized all over again—more so than when I relax in the evenings and get a full night's sleep. I have a purpose."

There was more to it than that. He went on.

"The thing about kids, the thing I didn't get until after these four were born, is that the joy and love and anticipation they bring to your life is like a magic spell." Hands folded between his knees, Joe studied the laces on his tennis shoes. "You go to bed tired, but you can't wait to get up in the morning and start all over again. To see what they're going to do that day. Will Thomas gain an ounce? Is Danny okay? Will Baby Grace smile when she sees me?"

He glanced up and stared when he saw the tears on Elise's cheeks.

"What?"

"Nothing." She brushed them aside. "Except that you've just proven what I've known for fifteen years."

"What's that?"

"You've got a lot more courage than I have."

AN ORDERLY POPPED HIS HEAD in the door and then left. The unit was quiet, peaceful, this late on Sunday.

"How can you say that?" Joe asked.

Elise moved over to the couch he sat on.

"Because all of this—these past months with you, the scares and the birth and the fact that Danny might be facing surgery—has shown me something about myself I'd never realized. I'm a coward."

"You're the strongest person I've ever met! My God, Elise, you fought pain worse than death, all alone, a little girl who'd just lost her mother, and the rest of her family. Thomas told me how they'd take bandages off and you'd bite back screams. That they'd put you through therapy that had tears rolling down your cheeks and you never said a word."

"I'm a survivor. I know that. I endure. But until this week, I never risked opening my heart to anyone since the night of that fire. That's why I couldn't find a man to share my life with. Not because I had a fake face, but because I wouldn't risk loving and losing again."

Even now, she trembled with fear. So much could go wrong. If Danny needed surgery, they'd be putting a four-pound baby under general anesthetic, risking infection. And any of the babies could go into cardiac arrest, or quit breathing, or get hit by a car when they crossed a street sometime.

"Do you know, other than the babies now, I've never told anyone I loved them since I was eleven years old?"

"That's not true."

"I know it's hard to believe, but actually, yes, it is."

"Actually, no, it's not."

Elise stared at him. "What do you mean?" Did he have some inside scoop on her life that she was missing?

"Because one week and one day ago when you were about to give birth, in front of about ten other people, you told me you loved me."

Elise panicked. "I did?" Oh, God. What else had she said?

"You did."

"What did you do?"

"I told you I felt the same."

She shivered, but not from cold. Her entire body was shaking so hard her teeth chattered. And then Joe's arm was around her shoulders, pulling her into his warmth.

"You just said that to spare me in front of all those people, didn't you?"

"I said it because it's true."

Turning her head against his shoulder, she looked up at him. "It is?"

"Yeah." He didn't seem all that upset about the idea.

"I have four kids."

"I love all four of them."

The nurse came in, asking if they wanted to help bathe the babies, and Elise, the coward, took the excuse to escape.

JOE WAS ALMOST ASLEEP that night, the covers keeping out the December chill that had permeated the old house in their absence, when he heard his door open.

"You awake?"

He was now. Completely. "Yeah."

"Can I come in?"

"Of course."

"I...um...just wanted to let you know that I'm going to call the clinic tomorrow and have them unseal the fertility records."

She hovered at the end of the bed, still wearing the sweat suit she'd had on all day.

Joe sat up, watching her with eyes adjusted to the darkness. "Sit." He indicated the bottom corner of the bed.

She sat.

And he wondered if all that talk earlier in the evening, the part about loving and opening up, had to do with someone other than him. Could she be hoping that Adam Fallow was the father of her children? Was that why she'd run off when he, Joe, had confessed his love for her?

And been chatty all the way home, with an urgent need to visit the bathroom as soon as they got there?

That she'd been avoiding personal conversation with him was obvious.

"Have you let Adam know your decision?"

"Not yet. I just made it."

And she'd come to him first. That had to be good, didn't it?

"The thing is, I've been living with this...I'm not sure what to call it...this *scarcity* mentality ever since I lost my family in the fire," she said slowly. "Like there's not enough love to go around for all of us. When, in truth, love is everywhere, and sharing it, while risky, also breeds it. And when you think there's not enough of it, you tend to hoard what little of it you have, which prevents it from spreading—and creates the scarcity of love you feared to begin with."

Even as tired as he was, he understood. He just didn't know exactly where this was leading. If it was leading anywhere.

"If it turns out that Adam is the babies' father, I don't have to give him fatherly rights to let him love them. He can be a doting uncle or something. It doesn't mean I lose any of their love. It just means their lives will be richer."

Joe thought *he* was the uncle.

"And if he's not," she went on, "then he has a chance to have children of his own and become a real father with a woman he loves."

Not Elise.

He thought about everything she'd said. About the things he'd learned about her over the past months. And the last of the dam within him broke wide open.

"I love you, Elise Richardson. More than I've ever loved anyone, anywhere, in my lifetime. I've wasted far too many years, and I need to share the rest of my life with you."

He ran out of words. And though he hated the silence that followed, he didn't regret speaking up.

"Are you asking me to marry you, Joe?" Her voice was hesitant in the darkness. She hadn't moved.

He considered her question. "Yes, I guess I am."

"Then I guess I accept."

Heart thudding in his chest, Joe slid out of bed, walked to her and pulled her up and into his arms.

"Say the words," he whispered, his lips an inch from hers.

"I just did. I'll marry you."

"Those are fine words, Elise, but not the ones I'm asking for. Tell me now, when you're completely sober and with your full faculties, what you told me last week when you were about to give birth."

He'd heard it in his head every day since. Analyzed the meaning behind those words in more ways than he'd have thought possible. She'd been speaking to someone else. Speaking out of her head. Speaking as a friend.

Speaking to her cats, which were right now curling about their ankles.

"I love you, Joe Bennett. I have since the day I first laid eyes on you. I was just too scared to realize it."

Her eyes brimmed with tears, but they didn't fall. Her hormones were settling down. She was getting back to her normal self.

And she loved him.

JOE PETITIONED to have the Richardson quads become the Bennett quads the same day he married their mommy, a full week before any of the babies had ever seen sunlight—there weren't any windows in the neonatal nursery.

And then, the first day they saw sunlight, they all squinted and closed their eyes. It was snowing. Danny felt the cold dots first, and cried. Thomas sucked in his breath. Ellen slept through, and Grace smiled.

Then all four of them slept in the van on the way home. There weren't many other cars out because it was Christmas Day and people were at home opening presents.

Ellen was the first to see the house they'd grow up in—and someday bring her own babies home to for Christmas. She, along with her brothers and sister, didn't get to see their room right away, though.

Daddy plopped little Santa hats on their heads, put them in little baskets under a huge tree that was all lit up with pretty colors, and took their picture.

The picture became famous. A card company bought it and it went all around the world with the caption Merry Christmas, Babies.

Mommy and Daddy got richer and had clients all over the country and lived happily ever after.

* * * * *

New York Times *bestselling author
Linda Lael Miller is back with a new romance
featuring the heartwarming McKettrick family
from* Silhouette Special Edition.

*SIERRA'S HOMECOMING
by Linda Lael Miller*

*On sale December 2006,
wherever books are sold.*

Turn the page for a sneak preview!

Soft, smoky music poured into the room.

The next thing she knew, Sierra was in Travis's arms, close against that chest she'd admired earlier, and they were slow dancing.

Why didn't she pull away?

"Relax," he said. His breath was warm in her hair.

She giggled, more nervous than amused. What was the matter with her? She was attracted to Travis, had been from the first, and he was clearly attracted to her. They were both adults. Why not enjoy a little slow dancing in a ranch-house kitchen?

Because slow dancing led to other things. She

took a step back and felt the counter flush against her lower back. Travis naturally came with her, since they were holding hands and he had one arm around her waist.

Simple physics.

Then he kissed her.

Physics again—this time, not so simple.

"Yikes," she said, when their mouths parted.

He grinned. "Nobody's ever said that after I kissed them."

She felt the heat and substance of his body pressed against hers. "It's going to happen, isn't it?" she heard herself whisper.

"Yep," Travis answered.

"But not tonight," Sierra said on a sigh.

"Probably not," Travis agreed.

"When, then?"

He chuckled, gave her a slow, nibbling kiss. "Tomorrow morning," he said. "After you drop Liam off at school."

"Isn't that…a little…soon?"

"Not soon enough," Travis answered, his voice husky. "Not nearly soon enough."

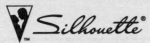

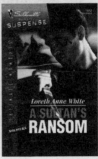

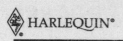

HARLEQUIN®

American ROMANCE®

IS PROUD TO PRESENT

COWBOY VET
by Pamela Britton

Jessie Monroe is the last person on earth
Rand Sheppard wants to rely on, but he needs
a veterinary technician—yesterday—and she's the
only one for hire. It turns out the woman who
destroyed his cousin's life isn't who Rand thought
she was. And now she's all he can think about!

"Pamela Britton writes the kind of
wonderfully romantic, sexy, witty romance
that readers dream of discovering
when they go into a bookstore."

—*New York Times* bestselling author
Jayne Ann Krentz

Cowboy Vet *is available from
Harlequin American Romance in December 2006.*

REQUEST YOUR FREE BOOKS!

2 FREE NOVELS PLUS 2 FREE GIFTS!

HARLEQUIN®

Super Romance®

Exciting, emotional, unexpected!

Harlequin® Historical
Historical Romantic Adventure!

Loyalty...or love?

LORD GREVILLE'S CAPTIVE
Nicola Cornick

He had previously come to Grafton
Manor to be betrothed to the beautiful
Lady Anne—but that promise was broken
with the onset of the English Civil War.
Now Lord Greville has returned as an
enemy, besieging the manor and holding
its lady prisoner.

His devotion to his cause is swayed by
his desire for Anne—he will have the
lady, and her heart.

Yet Anne has a secret that must be kept
from him at all costs....

On sale December 2006.
Available wherever Harlequin books are sold.

Silhouette®

Romantic
SUSPENSE

INTIMATE MOMENTS™

From *New York Times* bestselling author Maggie Shayne

When Selene comes to the aid of an unconscious stranger, she doesn't expect to be accused of harming him. The handsome stranger's amnesia doesn't help her cause either. Determined to find out what really happened to Cory, the two end up on an intense ride of dangerous pasts and the search for a ruthless killer.

DANGEROUS LOVER #1443
December 2006

Available wherever you buy books.

Visit Silhouette Books at www.eHarlequin.com

SIMMS27513

HARLEQUIN® *Romance*®

**From the Heart.
For the Heart.**

Get swept away into the Outback
with two of Harlequin Romance's
top authors.

Coming in December...

Claiming the
Cattleman's Heart
BY BARBARA HANNAY

And in January don't miss...

Outback Man Seeks Wife
BY MARGARET WAY

USA TODAY bestselling author

BARBARA McCAULEY

continues her award-winning series

S E C R E T S !

**A NEW BLACKHAWK FAMILY
HAS BEEN DISCOVERED...
AND THE SCANDALS ARE SET TO FLY!**

She touched him once and now
Alaina Blackhawk is certain horse rancher
DJ Bradshaw will be her first lover. But will
the millionaire Texan allow her to leave
once he makes her his own?

Blackhawk's Bond

On sale December 2006 (SD #1766)

Available at your favorite retail outlet.

Silhouette

nocturne™

Explore the dark and sensual
new realm of paranormal romance.

HAUNTED
BY LISA CHILDS

The first book in the riveting
new 3-book miniseries, Witch Hunt.

DEATH CALLS
BY CARIDAD PIÑEIRO

Darkness calls to humans,
as well as vampires...

*On sale December 2006,
wherever books are sold.*

SNNOV